THE DOCTOR'S STORY

The Doctor's Story

Mary Roberts Rinehart

Originally published in 1906.

ISBN: 979-8-3372-0195-5

This edition published in 2025 by MysteriousPress.com/Open Road Integrated Media, Inc.
180 Maiden Lane
New York, NY 10038
www.openroadmedia.com

INTRODUCTION

1906, the year *The Doctor's Story* originally appeared as a serial in *Watson's Magazine*, was a pivotal time in Mary Roberts Rinehart's development as a writer of long-form fiction. It was also around the time that she was honing her skills as a mystery writer, and the antecedents of many of the structural elements that came to be familiar to readers of her best-known books are present in *The Man in Lower Ten* and *The Doctor's Story*, serials which appeared within a few months of each other.

While the novel form of *The Man in Lower Ten* went on to become Rinehart's second bestseller three years later, *The Doctor's Story* was lost to time until the present, and has never even appeared in any of her several collections of shorter works. One can speculate why this was so, but 1906 was a particularly productive year for Rinehart as an emerging writer. She sold forty-six stories for a combined $1,842, about $64,000 today.[i] Three years earlier, the Rineharts were hit hard by the 1903 stock market crash, their savings wiped out, so it is possible that *The Doctor's Story* fell by the wayside as the family of five continued to recover.[ii]

---

i   "The Doctor's Story" sold for $225, about $7,800 today.

ii   In early 1903 the Rineharts were riding high with a house full of children and servants, a

It is not a mystery why she chose a doctor to be the protagonist in the *Watson's* serial. The story is told retrospectively—as is common in her stories—from the point of view of Dr. Carroll Pierce. Many of her stories took place in hospitals, and, of course, Hilda Adams—aka "Miss Pinkerton" of the eponymous mystery novel—was a nurse. Not only was Mary Roberts Rinehart the wife of a surgeon, but at one time she had aspired to a career in medicine herself.

As a teenager, Mamie Roberts (as she was then known) was both awed and intrigued by the sudden presence of C. Jane Vincent, M.D., on her street. As Rinehart recalled in her autobiography, *My Story*, "Just how long Doctor Vincent sat in her office and waited for patients I do not know, but gradually they began to drift in." Vincent's practice became "very successful," which struck Mamie's "small imagination" and prompted her to announce to her skeptical family that she, too, would train to become a doctor.

In the most unfortunate of coincidences in 1893, the year she might have started college, a financial crisis that would stretch into a four-year-long depression hit the country. "Now when I spoke of going to college there was a curious silence," she later recalled. "My music lessons ceased. One day I came home to find that my belongings had been shifted to my sister's room on the second floor, and that two strange men had rented the room on the third." In an act that would inform the rest of her life, she submitted three short stories to the local newspaper to improve the household finances. All three were accepted for the disappointing sum of one dollar each, after which she declared that her career as a woman of letters was over. Prophetically, her

---

busy medical practice, and a stock portfolio worth $12,000. By October, their entire savings were wiped out. Not only that, but they were $12,000 in debt as well. ("We might as well have owed twelve million," Mary recalled.)

Uncle John remarked that there was enough plot in one of the stories to make a book.

Medicine still intrigued her, so in August of 1893, she lied about her age and talked her way into the Pittsburgh Training School for Nurses at Homeopathic Hospital, an institution where surgeons who had learned their trade during the Civil War still insisted that maggots could cleanse a dirty wound. Her first assignment was to remove from the operating room a bucket containing a human foot. Though this incident shocked her, it did not make her physically ill. Still, hospital life made the study of medicine somewhat less romantic than the imagined ideal of Dr. Vincent's practice. Recalling her stint at the hospital's emergency ward, Rinehart wrote:

> One morning I came on duty to find the battered body of a man who had been beaten to death with an iron pipe. One cold evening that fall just before going off duty, I turned down the bed for a burly policeman, crying as though his heart would break, while he placed on it the body of a small newsboy, burned and dying from the fire he had built to keep himself warm. A woman was brought in slashed in thirty places with a knife by a jealous rival: a pretty woman. She recovered.

She also grew to learn the hypocrisy and heartlessness of those of supposedly superior moral character, especially when it came to suffering. Caring for a cancerous mother and her love child, she recalled:

> She had had a child and had had the courage to acknowledge it, so she was dying alone. Ever since that time, I have felt the cruelty and bitterness of our attitude toward the unmarried mother and her child. How stupid we are, that two wrongs can ever make a right.

In her early days at the hospital, she also became acquainted with the "rather severe" Dr. Stanley Marshall Rinehart. Dr. Rinehart, a very young (twenty-five years old in 1894) surgeon and thus probably not of the maggots-as-antiseptic school of thought, was known not only for his skill with the knife but also his perfectionism and fierce temper.

Their acquaintance grew into a friendship, their friendship into a romance. Ever the risk-taker, Mary flouted hospital policy by agreeing to an engagement with a fellow staff member. Very soon thereafter the hospital's chief engineer stumbled upon a tryst between them and word of their relationship spread like an epidemic. Confronted with the facts by the hospital board, Dr. Rinehart responded to their accusations by yelling at them and telling them that it was none of their business. With the meek request that Mary not flaunt her engagement by wearing a ring, the board simply "went away."

Mary Ella Roberts became Mary Roberts Rinehart on April 21, 1896. After intervals of illness and residual exhaustion brought on from her two years of work at the hospital, she found her first child forming in her belly in December of that year. Because Dr. Rinehart ran his practice out of the first floor of their home, Mary served as his secretary and even assisted in minor medical procedures, which kept her abreast of the latest developments in the field, at least until her third and final child was born and motherhood became her priority

Mary's prior medical experience informed *The Doctor's Story* in several ways. Her knowledge of pharmaceuticals plays a role in the mysterious switching-out of medications for Pierce's patient, Henry St. John, who suffers from seizures. She understood the protocol for dealing with a poison victim in order to portray the young Dr. Pierce, a progressive in the field of medicine in defiance of his aging mentor, Jamieson.

St. John concurs by requesting Pierce "bring [in] one of the younger men, one a little more progressive than Jamieson. These older men don't give me a ghost of a chance; now let's see what a younger man can do." Such a doctor, Carter, arrives. "One of the new men," Pierce explains, "an aggressive kind of fellow who doesn't know the word conservatism, and who isn't hampered by precedent." Echoes of the kind of hospital politics Stanley Rinehart encountered at Pittsburgh Homeopathic resonate here, a conflict truly drawn from life.[i]

Those familiar with Rinehart's *The Man in Lower Ten* will be surprised and delighted to see the return of Wilson Budd Hotchkiss, or "Hotchkiss," in *The Doctor's Story*. In most of her mysteries, Rinehart leavened horror and suspense with humor and romance, and Hotchkiss was the means by which she introduced both. As described by the late Jan Cohn in her superb biography, *Improbably Fiction: The Life of Mary Roberts Rinehart*, Hotchkiss is a "little man," who "carries around a notebook, searches for clues, tails suspects, and comes up with astonishing inductions." As Cohn describes his eccentric contributions in *The Man in Lower Ten*:

> He introduces himself to Blakely with the announcement, "I use the induction method originated by Poe and followed since with such success by Conan Doyle." His culminating act of detection comes late in the novel when he boasts of having discovered the missing

---

i   By 1910 Stanley Rinehart found his practice going stale, so he decided to take some time away and study diseases of the heart and lung in Vienna, Austria, a mecca for medical learning at the time. Mary was by now a wealthy woman and insisted that the entire family accompany him. Dr. Rinehart reluctantly agreed. When the United States entered World War I in 1917, through her influence in Washington, D.C., Mary arranged a commission for Stan in the Army Medical Corps. Major Rinehart served with distinction and earned the couple a place at Arlington National Cemetery, though Mary's devout patriotism and pioneering work as a war correspondent may have also contributed to the honor.

Sullivan and sent the police to apprehend him. "It's a great day in modern detective methods," he chirped. "While the police have been guarding houses and standing with their mouths open waiting for clues to fall in and choke them, we have pieced together, bit by bit—a fabric." He is interrupted by the arrival of the police and their captive. Alas, Hotchkiss has not been tailing Sullivan but Blakely's own confidential clerk.

As Cohn further points out, Rinehart occasionally spoofed the mystery or detective novel "as she wrote one," noting that the blockbuster *The Circular Staircase* was originally intended as satire.

That Hotchkiss should reappear in *The Doctor's Story* begs the question of whether Rinehart was trying out the "little man" as a recurring character meant to bring levity to a story characterized by screams in the night, shadowy characters, attempted murder, and mysterious disappearances. Certainly Hotchkiss does that with his amateur sleuthing about cases in far-off cities that are none of his business.

Perhaps Hotchkiss was being tried out in the manner of a Miss Marple, though the Agatha Christie mainstay came along some twenty-one years after Hotchkiss's debut in *The Man in Lower Ten* and Hotchkiss was more Inspector Clouseau than the venerable Marple. Regardless, after *The Doctor's Story*, Hotchkiss never appeared again in a Rinehart mystery, ending the experiment. A more enduring recurring character, Letitia Carberry, would be one of Rinehart's most beloved subjects.[i]

---

i It's doubtful Jan Cohn would have known about Hotchkiss's reappearance in *The Doctor's Story* or she surely would have mentioned it in *Improbable Fiction*. Though Cohn was familiar with all of Rinehart's novels and parsed many short stories to investigate how events in Rinehart's life might have informed them, Rinehart's body of work was huge and impossible to master.

Hotchkiss is also the target of an unlikely romance in *The Doctor's Story*, courting St. John's nurse, Miss Martin, after earlier having urged Pierce to fire her out of a suspicion of foul play, yet another bumbling "induction."

Romances were other devices frequently used as digressions from the main plots, and they often became subplots themselves. The romantic tension in *The Doctor's Story* is between Pierce and the comely Georgia Ellis as Pierce tries to peel back the layers of secrecy and scandal that consume her. The denouement of their passion is typical Rinehart, as all the loose ends are tied up or otherwise accounted for in the final pages of the story. As the editor of *Munsey's*, Bob Davis, once advised her, ". . . remember always to keep the lovers apart until the last chapter."

The setting for *The Doctor's Story* is "the heart of the Maine mountains," as Carter describes it, "twelve hours from town and an hour from a railroad." That Rinehart would set the story in so remote a locale makes St. John's estate, Laurelcrest, a mysterious character in itself with its towers, its creepy basements, and labyrinth of rooms, alcoves, and corridors, where a trick of the light can betray ghosts and other apparitions. The dark woods come right up to the one side of the house, where "the forest trees rustled against the eaves; here the pheasant drummed, unmolested, and gray squirrels chased each other under the very windows."

The description of the setting is all the more admirable because it is unlikely Rinehart had ever visited Maine when she wrote the story. For Dr. and Mrs. Rinehart, a holiday away from their home in Pittsburgh would usually mean a trip to New York City to take in the theater or for Mary to call on publishers.

If one puts the clues together, Rinehart has no doubt set her story near what is now Baxter State Park, Maine's most mountainous area, which became accessible by rail spur at the turn of the twentieth century. St. John's mention of a nearby mountain named "Old Baldy" could be an oblique reference to Maine's highest mountain, Katahdin.

The village, Carson. in *The Doctor's Story* is fictional. Though one can find Carson as a neighborhood in the town of Woodland in northernmost Maine, the topography is flat and there was no train service to that part of the state until 1911. So, the Maine of Rinehart's imagination was probably based on something she had read or heard about, and the twelve-hour train trip to get there places the city of departure anywhere from New York to Pittsburgh.

As it happened, Rinehart's familiarity with and affection for Maine would come later in life, and Maine was the setting for life imitating art in a nearly fatal way for her. For two decades starting in 1915, Rinehart had been spending her summers at Eaton's Ranch in Wyoming. But, by the mid-1930s, it became no longer advisable to subject her weak heart to the ranch's 6,000-foot altitude.[i]

Instead, she was drawn to Bar Harbor and its colony of writers, artists, and musicians, who found the area conducive to work and contemplation and not just idleness or recreation. "The idea that [Bar Harbor] was purely social has always been a mistake," she insisted in *My Story*. In fact, work became a necessity for her when in 1937 she bought a house in Bar Harbor on the cheap but in need of much repair. "There was only one answer, of course," she wrote, "going back to work."[ii]

---

i   She was by now also a widow, Dr. Rinehart having died in 1932.

ii   Not that anyone should feel sorry for her. She still owned a large apartment in New York City and wintered at exclusive Useppa Island in Florida, and also maintained a modest household staff.

Rinehart owned the Bar Harbor estate until 1947, when the "Great Bar Harbor Fire" destroyed over seventy houses that, including hers (she had by that time returned to New York). However, something happened to her the previous summer that was straight out of a Mary Roberts Rinehart crime novel, and which was an eerie echo of the crescendo of events in *The Doctor's Story*.

In the early 1920s, while she and her husband were living in Washington, D.C., she decided to hire a cook, since their ample apartment could accommodate both a kitchen and a dining room. "One day a tall Filipino [named Reyes] presented himself," she wrote, describing him as "dignified and quiet," with "excellent references." She hired him and, over time, Reyes became "a czar in the domestic staff," for the next twenty-five years. The Rineharts were so loyal to Reyes that when Reyes married an Irishwoman named Peggy, she was hired as their parlor maid. By the early 1940s, however, Rinehart had started to notice disturbing changes in Reyes's health and behavior. "Off and on for five years I had him under medical care," she wrote, "and twice I had sent him to hospitals." Equally as worrisome to Rinehart was that Reyes had started to become "race conscious" with all the resentments that entails, though she claimed she "never thought of his color."

In the summer of 1947, after Rinehart hired both a chauffeur and butler, Reyes's jealousy and resentment crossed the line into madness at around noon one Saturday. He had given his notice the day before but, since he had threatened quitting once or twice before, only later to say he had not meant it, Rinehart expected the same recantation. But, it did not come this time, and worse still, his wife Peggy had refused to leave with him. So before lunch that day, Reyes, as a dresser "the most meticulous of men," appeared before his employer in mere shirtsleeves.

"Why Reyes," she asked, "where is your coat?" Drawing closer, he replied, "This is my coat," and pulled a revolver from his trousers and fired at her from point-blank range. But the gun misfired, giving his intended victim time to push him aside and flee through the house in search of help.

But the chaos was just getting started. "I knew then that I had a maniac on my hands," she wrote, "and that he still meant to kill me." As luck would have it—or as she put it, "By the Providence of God"—her chauffeur, Ted Falkenstrom, was in the pantry, and another of her staff, Margaret, was in the kitchen as Reyes continued to chase Mary, gun still raised. Falkenstrom was able to knock him down while Margaret seized the gun. But Reyes was able to escape and, while Falkenstrom disposed of the gun, Reyes came after Mary again wielding three carving knives as she hurried to the library to phone the police. As he was about to strike, Falkensrom, this time joined by the gardener, was able to subdue him and wrest the knives away, but not without some bad cuts to the chauffeur's hands. A policeman arrived shortly thereafter, and Reyes "went quietly with him, not looking at any of us." Later that night Reyes hanged himself in his jail cell.

As in a Rinehart murder mystery, the terror was offset by its lighter moments, especially when viewed in retrospect. At the first sign of trouble the newly-hired butler had hightailed it out the door and hitchhiked into town rather than come to his employer's aid. And as Mary made her way down the back hall to the library and the telephone, she noticed a tall boy at the door and stopped. As she describes the encounter in *My Story*:

'I understand you need someone to help your gardener,' he said politely.

I stared at him, hardly seeing him.

'Young man,' I said, 'you'll have to come back later. There is a man in here trying to kill me.'

I do not know what happened to him. He disappeared out of my life and never came back, but I have often wondered what he made of that situation. I think, however, that he must have told the gardener all was not well, for the latter appeared later. Just in time, as it happens.

The attempted murder of Mary Roberts Rinehart led the headlines in the early summer of 1947, though *Time* magazine relegated the incident to its gossipy "People" section in its June 30 issue. "After . . . years of turning out imaginative whodunits," the article snarked, "[Rinehart] found herself . . . face to face with reality. Scene: the library of the twenty-four-room Rinehart mansion in fashionable Bar Harbor . . . (probably the location of her murderous *The Yellow Room*)." After describing the attack, the article asked, and the seventy-year-old writer responded: "The motive: Confessed Author Rinehart, who has written many a tale about derangement and crime: 'I can't think of what . . .'"

One year before the events that defined her final days in Maine, *Life* magazine had published a respectful look-back at Mary Roberts Rinehart's forty-year career, claiming that for thirty-five of those years, "she has been America's best-selling lady author." It is doubtful that she would have ever foreseen, or dreamed of, this outcome as she worked to write her family out of debt in 1906, but necessity helped to inspire the discipline and creativity that were essential for her later successes.

Though overlooked since its debut in *Watson's Magazine*, *The Doctor's Story* is in retrospect a bellwether of what was to come.

Rick Rinehart

THE DOCTOR'S STORY

CHAPTER ONE

I saw Hotchkiss the other day at the club, and he brought back to me vividly the strange experiences we had together at Laurelcrest—strange that is, to look back upon. At the time we would have characterized them more strongly.

"Do you remember what Carter said?" Hotchkiss asked, as he filled out his slip. And I remembered. Carter was used up, like the rest of us, that last morning at Laurelcrest, and he made only one remark, to my recollection, during breakfast. "Talk about the excitement of city life!" he said. "Well, for pure, hair-lifting business, give me the heart of the Maine mountains, twelve hours from town and an hour from a railroad."

With Carter, however, the events at Laurelcrest were only incidental to a busy and not unexciting career. To me they were much more, altering, as they did, the entire course of my life. Had I never left the hospital to accompany Mr. Henry St. John to his country estate I would not have missed the Berlin clinics, and today I should probably be a specialist on the eye and ear, spending my mornings in luxurious offices and my afternoons playing golf, instead of a hard-working general practitioner, using two horses a day in relays, and sleeping with one ear open for the telephone and the other for the office bell.

Everybody interested in surgical matters knows Dr. Jamieson. When he announced that Henry St. John's case was an incurable one, the other members of the staff proceeded to agree with him, and so great was his reputation that when St. John, frenzied at the thought of leaving his young wife, sent for consultants from other cities, they heard Jamieson's verdict with respect, and acquiesced in it. As this account of the strange occurrences at Laurelcrest is meant for the lay mind, I need not go into details. It is sufficient to say that the trouble was a creeping paralysis of the right leg, with intervals of unconsciousness, which Jamieson and the other men who ought to know declared epileptic in origin, while I, Carrol Pierce, numbering not as many years of life as Jamieson had to his credit in the profession, ventured to differ from their diagnosis, and was properly snubbed for my pains.

St. John was growing daily more anemic and emaciated. It was late in October when he finally decided to leave the hospital and go to Laurelcrest, taking with him the middle-aged nurse who had cared for him since early summer, and myself. I think he took me for companionship; certainly he had no hope of my being very useful in a professional way, but he had seemed to like me, and I felt a warm admiration for him in return. He was perhaps a dozen years older than I, very handsome, even now in his emaciation, with finely chiseled features, a sensitive, thin-lipped mouth and a square jaw.

He had been married a year before to a Southern girl, a Kentuckian, as fair as the proverbial Southern girl is dark—a tall, willowy girl, whose attention had been unremitting during his illness. His devotion to her was pitiful, and, with what I have always considered a mistaken idea of kindness, he had refused to inform her of his real condition. In fact, he had enlisted us all, staff, internes and nurses, in the deception, and she came to the hospital daily, with her arms full of flowers and her face glowing with smiles, while we who knew the real state of things looked on and wondered.

Then a queer thing happened. Mrs. St. John suddenly refused to go to Laurelcrest. There was a week or so during which St. John argued in vain, and during which, before our very eyes, his wife grew paler and thinner, offering one inadequate excuse after another and persisting in her refusal. Then St. John, choosing to treat the matter as a whim, took affairs into his own hands, made arrangements to go to Laurelcrest and told his wife, gently but firmly, only a few days before the journey.

Miss Martin, the nurse, reported an uncomfortable interview, and the hospital people, being staunch allies of St. John, resented it. Knowing what I do now, I do not wonder at her unwillingness, and as she was ignorant of her husband's real condition, perhaps we judged her too harshly.

The afternoon of the day set for the journey I had a long interview with St. John and when I finally left the room I had much to think over. St. John saw in his wife's refusal to go to Laurelcrest a deeper, more subtle origin than a capricious dislike for the place, and he asked my assistance in helping him to solve the mystery.

"She must not even suspect my condition," he finished. "We will tell her at the last, but we can give her a few months, not of happiness, for she is not happy, but of ignorance. I have no qualms about discovering this secret, whatever it is, for I cannot resign myself to—what may happen, knowing that she has some trouble which she is concealing from me. We are going to be conspirators, Pierce, conspiring for the happiness of the best woman in the world."

There was nothing eventful about the journey. We reached the station nearest to Laurelcrest sometime in the night, and our special car was switched onto the side-track until morning.

Mr. St. John was very quiet, and the nurse had no occasion to rouse me, so it was eight o'clock when I wakened. It was the first time for two years that I had not opened my eyes to the dull gray of my hospital room, and to the all-pervading odor of drugs and antiseptics. It was bewildering, for a moment, to find instead the polished wood of the sleeper, with glimpses outside of towering pine-capped ridges, and to breathe air that consisted of oxygen and nitrogen in proper proportions, instead of the sickly combination of smoke, unconsumed gases and foul exhalations which we of the cities dignify as the atmosphere.

We were to breakfast in the car before starting on our drive to Laurelcrest, and I stepped in to see my patient on my way to the dining room. He was propped up in his berth, looking out at the black line of the hills thrusting their unwieldy masses against the gray-blue of the sky, and for a man who had passed a quiet night he was singularly worn and pale. As I entered, he motioned me to close the stateroom door, and I did so.

"Did Miss Martin tell you I slept?" he asked, when I had sat down beside him. "She said you were quiet."

"I was," he said. "Do you see that road over there, doctor?" I nodded affirmatively.

"The moon was late last night. At first the swish of the river beside the track made me sleepy, but about midnight a freight train puffed up the mountain with a fearful racket, and I found myself wide-awake. I watched the moon come up behind Old Baldy, that dome-shaped mountain over there, and then I saw a man come rapidly along the road toward the car. Had there been two of them I might have feared a hold-up, for Carson, the nearest town, is four miles away, but it seemed ridiculous under the circumstances. So I lay still and watched him for a while. He was smoking—I could see the spark as he came near—and after a bit he threw the cigar away and stopped. It was perfectly dark here in the car, so he could not see me."

"The porter, perhaps, taking a moonlight stroll," I suggested.

"It was a queer hour for a walk," said St. John dryly.

"Did you waken Miss Martin?"

"Not for a while. The man came up to the car and stood staring at it. Then he began to walk around it, looking up at the windows as he passed. Then he stopped coming and I thought I heard voices, but when I finally got Miss Martin awake enough to comprehend what I wanted, he had disappeared. She looked around and saw nothing, but as the moon was covered with clouds he might have been near without being seen."

"That is nothing," I said reassuringly. "Some tramp, probably, hunting for a place to sleep."

"It was not a tramp. Why should Mrs. St. John talk to a tramp at that hour of the night?"

"Are you sure she did?" I asked, startled.

"Not only that," he said grimly, "but I am convinced that he was concealed in some part of the car while Miss Martin was looking around. I could hear muffled voices, as if both Mrs. St. John and her cousin, Miss Ellis, were talking, with now and then a heavier voice, and it was fully half an hour before I saw him go back up the road again."

"It sounds strange enough, I admit," I said, as I got up, "but there is probably some natural explanation that will clear the thing up in a hurry. Things have a tendency to look mysterious on a moonlit night."

But although St. John smiled faintly I felt that he realized, as I did, that it must be a matter of some moment that would bring a visitor to our car in that remote place at such an unseasonable hour. And when I finally went to my breakfast it was with the conviction that St. John had been right, and that there had been some mysterious reason for his wife's repugnance to Laurelcrest.

The two ladies had almost finished when I went into the small dining-room. Mrs. St. John presented me to her cousin, Miss Ellis, who inspected me rather closely, I thought. For my part, perhaps I looked a little longer than necessary at the girl across the table, for there are some women at whom one glance seems to demand another. It was that way with Miss Ellis.

Between wondering whether her eyes were blue or gray, and debating whether her hair was brown or red, and whether it was either, how she came to have such black, finely-drawn brows—well, I got on slowly with my breakfast.

I had more courage where women are concerned in those days than I have now. For one thing I knew less about them. Today I should hesitate before the step I took that morning at breakfast, but twenty-six takes only itself seriously, so I plunged into my grapefruit and into trouble with equal calmness.

"Fairly," I said, in reply to a query of Mrs. St. John's. "I always sleep in the mountains."

"I slept unusually well myself," she said, pulling down the veil which had been turned up over her hat. "It is so still here."

For just an instant Miss Ellis glanced at me, then she looked quickly away. Mrs. St. John's face belied her words. Her heavy eyes looked as if she had kept vigil all night.

"It is odd," I went on, "but I had a queer kind of hallucination last night. It was shadowy on my side of the car, but once or twice I could have sworn that a man passed under my window, looking up at it as he went by."

I reached over for more sugar for my grapefruit, glancing carelessly at Miss Ellis as I did so. To my utter amazement she started guiltily and flushed crimson. I was too late to see Mrs. St. John's face, for she rose abruptly and went to the window. But the action seemed significant, and in the strained silence that followed I wondered what it all meant. What man would seek our car, four miles from a village on a lonely side-track in the mountains, and hold stealthy conversation with one or both of the two ladies in the party? What was the motive for concealing his visit from Mrs. St. John and myself? And what share had Miss Ellis in what had seemed to be a family skeleton?

I did not allow my meditations to interfere with my meal. The mountain air had made me hungry, and the chef was an expert, like most railroad cooks. The ladies left me to finish alone, Miss Ellis going to attend to the handbags, Mrs. St. John going to her husband. After the meal was over I stepped down onto the cinder path beside the track and looked around me. At my feet the little river swirled and foamed, breaking into spray that the wind dashed in my face. I walked round the car, my eyes on the ground, looking for any possible clue to the midnight visitor.

There were muddy footprints here and there on the ties, but I was too inexperienced to learn much from them. I did find and pick up, however, a half-smoked cigarette, which lay between the tracks at the end of the car, and whose paper cover looked fresh and new. I examined it closely. It was an Egyptian cigarette, of a fair grade, and I dropped it into my pocket; possibly it would give me something to work from.

I walked up the road a dozen yards or so and was rewarded by finding another similar piece.

It was too late to look farther. The carriage and baggage wagon from Laurelcrest were coming slowly down the mountain road, the latter with a creaking of brakes and rattling of chairs, so I turned back to the car. I tipped the porter to the limit of my means. Then I had an inspiration.

"Here, George," I said, pulling out a box of cigarettes and

proffering them, "I'll give you these if you smoke; I'm not smoking for a while."

George grinned and shook his head.

"Thank you, sir," he said civilly, pocketing my dollar, "but it's against the regulations to smoke on duty, sir, and besides, I can't never smoke cigarettes. Seems like they give me the headache."

So it had not been George who dropped the half-burnt cigarettes around the car!

It was not difficult to move Mr. St. John to Laurelcrest. We had telegraphed to have the omnibus sent over, and Miss Martin and I contrived a comfortable bed on the floor between the seats. At Mr. St. John's request we sent the two ladies ahead in the carriage to have everything ready for our arrival. It was one of his many pitiful ruses to keep his wife in ignorance of his condition.

"It will kill her, doctor, if she sees that I have to be carried," he explained.

"Tell her to go ahead and get things ready—hot water bags— anything, but don't let her see how helpless I am."

Miss Martin sniffed. She had little sympathy with the finer sensibilities, and, personally, I think she took it as an affront that her patient's wife would not or could not see his real condition.

"That's the way with these wealthy women," she said to me that morning as the carriage drove off, Mrs. St. John waving her hand and smiling at the face in the car window, that watched her with an answering smile. "They are so self-centered, so selfish, that they can't see the things that are plain to everybody else."

In my heart I began to agree with her. None but a self-engrossed woman or a woman with some secret grief would have been so blind. Dr. Jamieson himself had said that had she ever questioned him closely he was afraid he would have told her the truth, but that she had limited her inquiries to the barest generalities. And yet it was difficult to reconcile her indifference—abstraction more nearly describes it—with her evident love for her husband.

The road was a bad one. We went slowly, driving around the rocks that cropped out every place and fording a couple of small streams that crossed the road. At one of the crossings I was astonished to see Miss Ellis standing on the plank which formed a bridge. As I glanced out, she called to me.

"We're almost there, doctor," she said, "and Mrs. St. John suggested that I should take you over the hill here to get the most imposing view of the place. Do you care to walk?"

"Yes, go," said St. John. "It's better walking than riding."

I got out gladly enough. I hadn't yet solved the question of Miss Ellis's eyes, and the hill looked steep enough to promise an opportunity to assist her at difficult places. Oddly enough, however, her manner was constrained and stiff. We climbed for a few minutes—long enough for me to discover that my companion neither desired nor needed assistance, and that, however friendly my feelings for her, her attitude to me was distinctly hostile. The road below had disappeared behind a line of rocks before Miss Ellis stopped and faced me.

"I brought you here, Dr. Pierce, because I wanted to talk to you, or rather, because I have a message for you from Mrs. St. John."

She was flushed with the exercise and her hair was loosened just sufficiently to blow out around her face in soft little waves. But she looked at me with eyes that were openly defiant.

"I am going to ask a favor of you," she said, in tones that were anything but supplicating. "My cousin, Mrs. St. John, would like, for the present, at least, to conceal a certain thing from her husband, and she needs your cooperation. Will you help her?"

"I should like to know first what I am promising," I said.

She looked at me angrily. "Will it do if I say that it is something that would do your patient harm to know? That it would worry and excite him needlessly?"

I thought for a moment, feeling very uncomfortable under her half-contemptuous glance. How was I going to help St. John if I promised at the very outset to conceal things from him? And yet, how could I refuse what seemed a natural if somewhat unusual request?

"Very well," I said, yielding as gracefully as I could. "I will promise, although as a rule, Miss Ellis, it's been policy to help a wife conceal things from her husband, or vice versa. If the secret gets out, both of them are apt to turn on the other fellow."

She looked relieved then and even deigned to smile a little.

"It's really not much of a conspiracy," she said. "It is simply this. Mr. St. John has always disliked—well, even more than disliked—my cousin, his wife's brother. It seemed to be a mutual antagonism and we gave up trying to mend things between them long ago. Shall we walk on? It is not steep now, and I can talk to you as we go."

We moved slowly on, side by side now, along a faint path through the woods which covered the hill. Insensibly, now that she had gained her point, Miss Ellis's reserve was melting, and something like cordiality was taking its place.

"Well, things have been happening lately which have necessitated that Frank—Frank Ellis is his name—that Frank should go into retirement for a while. We are Kentuckians, you know, and things are queer down there, politically. So, as Frank has no place else to go, his sister sent him here to Laurelcrest. He is here now and we do not wish Mr. St. John to know it. Do you understand now?"

"I understand," I said. It was very plausible, very true, no doubt. What's more natural than that this young Ellis, involved in a political feud, had been hounded from his state and sought temporary refuge in this isolated place? And yet—I did not believe the girl had told me all the truth. "Things have been happening"—that was indefinite enough. "Queer, politically"—yes, but I had heard of no one named Ellis sufficiently in disgrace with his party to have to leave the state. Well, I had given my word, anyhow.

"That explains the visit to the car last night?" I said suddenly. The girl drew herself up and looked at me steadily.

"What visit?" she asked. And I saw that I had reached the limit of her confidence. They had told me something, of necessity; if there was anything beyond this, I was not to know.

I did not repeat the remark. Miss Ellis led the way quickly, with a free, swinging gait that was wonderfully graceful and easy. She was tall, almost my own height indeed, but girlishly slim, with a breadth of shoulder that promised a magnificent maturity. Just now, however, she seemed very young, very troubled, in spite of her hauteur, and I had a crazy longing to pat her shoulder and tell her I was sorry they were in trouble—that I appreciated her loyalty to her cousin, and couldn't I help in some way? But I, too, owed loyalty and that to my patient, which reminded me of the omnibus and its pitiful freight.

"Are we nearly there?" I asked. "I should like to oversee the moving of Mr. St. John."

"We are almost there," she said. "Doctor, you may deceive his wife, but you cannot deceive me. Harry St. John is worse."
She stopped and looked at me, her eyes almost level with my own. "Why do you think so?" I asked noncommittally.

"It is confidence for confidence, is it?" she said shrewdly. "I'm sorry, but the confidence is not mine to give."

"Nor mine," I answered gravely.

CHAPTER TWO

The house was all I had been led to expect, and more. Built of stone, in a country where such building material cropped out of every hillside, it spread irregularly over an immense area, its dull green shingles and soft grays melting harmoniously into the grays and greens of the landscape. There were wide verandas of stone, cool and shady, and level lawns with quaint, conventional flower beds and pergolas. Around three sides of the house the landscape gardener had done his best; a little river had been bridged with a massiveness of stone out of all proportion to its size, and was still abloom its entire length with flaming red and gold nasturtiums. But the fourth side, at the west wing of the house, had been left untouched. Here, separated by a hedge from their cultivated sisters, the forest trees rustled against the eaves; here the pheasant drummed, unmolested, and gray squirrels chased each other under the very windows.

It was in this wing that St. John had his apartments, and it was here that we carried him, carefully as we could, and laid him on a couch in his dressing room, near a window. My apartments were at the other end of the house in the east, while Mrs. St. John and Miss Ellis occupied the rooms which faced the north and main exposure. At the angles where the wings oined the house were squat towers, rounded, with small, high windows. Inside, the architects had used these towers to advantage. On the lower floor they formed cushioned and seated recesses off the immense square hall, with hanging lamps of wrought iron, and teakwood tabourets. In Mr. St. John's apartments, and in my own, they were lined with bookshelves under the high windows, with a heavy, square writing-table, and were separated from the dressing rooms only by portieres. As to the floor above, I could only suppose a similar use.

I found my clothes unpacked and put away, and surmised that Jones, Mr. St. John's man, was looking after me. My half-dozen medical books—an anatomy, a pathology, two *materiamedicas*, a little quiz book and a "Brain Surgery"—were arranged in lonely grandeur on the shelves in the tower room.

It was time for luncheon, and I straightened myself up a little, luxuriating, after my eighteen-inch stationary washstand in the hospital, in the big, tiled bathroom which adjoined my bedroom.

Then I looked out of the window.

There were two people on the stone bridge, a man and a woman. I could not see her features, but I recognized the height and erect poise of Miss Ellis. The man had his back toward me, and was leaning over the railing, listening, evidently, for the girl was in animated conversation. Once I thought she stamped her foot, but I could not be certain. Of one thing, however, there could be no doubt: I was wildly, unreasonably jealous of this indolent stranger, this cousin and brother whom two good women were shielding at such cost to themselves.

The people on the bridge turned and came toward me, and I had a good opportunity to study the man's face. He was dark—Franklin, at the hospital, used to say that no villain is ever fair and very tall. Taller than I, I fancied, but more slender, with shoulders that stooped a trifle, and a skin of an unhealthy yellow; and yet, in spite of it all, he was a handsome fellow, with a clean-cut, prominent nose and dark eyes.

He seemed uneasy under the girl's harangue. He put his hands in his pockets and took them out again; took off the motor cap he wore and put it on, all the time looking every way but at her.

When she ceased, however, and by that time they were close beneath my window, he raised his eyes—heavy-lidded eyes they were, and sleepy—and looked at her. There was no mistaking the glance. It was love that she saw there, love so evident that I, who had been a skeptic as to the tender passion—we are all skeptics until we get hit—I knew it at once, and burned with wrath and jealousy.

We were introduced at the luncheon table, and I received his indolent handshake with one equally unenthusiastic. We were not an animated party at the table. Mrs. St. John was silent and distraite, eating little and crumbling her bread with nervous fingers. Mr. Ellis sat opposite his cousin and devoured her with his eyes, while I carried on a labored monologue about the scenery and the air.

"I'm glad you think it is bracing, doctor," Miss Ellis said once, a little spitefully. "You're just like the natives. They talk air instead of politics, and spell it with a capital at each end and one in the middle."

I subsided after that, and luncheon ended gloomily enough. Ellis slouched out of the room and disappeared for the afternoon. Mrs. St. John went to her husband's room, to allow the nurse a little freedom, and I went to the big library and prepared to spend an hour or so with my old friends on the shelves. It was there that Miss Martin found me, her cap over her ear with excitement, her portly figure swelling with indignation.

CHAPTER THREE

"I am sorry to disturb you, doctor," she said, her voice shaking with suppressed anger, "but I want to ask you to define my duties in this house. I realize fully—I am a woman of sense, doctor—I realize my obligations to you and to my patient. But when my patient's wife comes to me and asks me to help her deceive her husband, as fine a man as ever I met—well, I think there's something wrong!"

"You are not very clear, Miss Martin," I said. "What is it she wants you to do?"

"Well, it isn't much, doctor, after all, and it isn't only one thing. But something queer happened in the train last night and I've been puzzling over it all day. You see, Mr. St. John slept the early part of the night and I dozed, too. About midnight he wakened and I gave him some water. I didn't go to sleep again, but I kept very quiet and I suppose he thought me sleeping. I could see that he was awake. He raised himself on his elbow once or twice and looked out at the moon, but didn't call me for anything. After a while I heard the knob of the stateroom door turn and someone came in. At first I thought it was Mrs. St. John, but it wasn't. It was her cousin, Miss Ellis. She stood inside the door for a minute and looked at us. I closed my eyes and pretended to be sleeping, and Mr. St. John may have been dozing—I don't know."

I got up and softly closed the library door; I thought I heard footsteps outside. "Now go on," I said, "but softly."

"Well, you know the way I've been preparing things at night, in the hospital. I always put the medicines on a stand, with a night light, and fix a little tray with my hypodermic ready to use, and the alcohol and soluble tablets ready. I fixed it that way last night in the stateroom, and Miss Ellis went right to that tray. I watched her move the light and examine one after the other of the hypodermic vials, but when she turned to go my eyes were shut and she slipped out quietly again. My corner was dark, but I could see Mr. St. John plainly and he was wide awake. Probably he had feigned sleep, as I had done. But I'm all upset today, doctor. There's something wrong here—there's murder in the very air! Why, every one of those vials was loaded with poison!"

I had a decided foreboding of evil myself. I got up and paced the room slowly, trying to find some easy, natural solution for Miss Ellis's action. There seemed to be no explanation. Had she or Mrs. St. John been ill, they could easily have aroused Miss Martin or myself. There would have been no necessity for concealment.

"Have you any idea what drug she took?" I asked, stopping in front of Miss Martin.

"I cannot be certain. I did not dare to get up at once, for fear Mr. St. John might suspect that I had seen what had occurred. He called me, toward morning, and I examined the tray then. The strychnia lay apart from the others, but I cannot be certain that any had been taken."

"What did the other vials contain?"

"Just the contents of my hypodermic case, doctor. There are four vials in all, strychnia, apomorphia, nitroglycerine and morphia."

"It's utterly inexplicable," I admitted, "but we can be certain of one thing, Miss Martin—neither Miss Ellis nor Mrs. St. John would harm anyone. I am sure of it."

"I'm not," she said firmly. "Pardon me for contradicting you, doctor, but I do not understand Mrs. St. John at all, and I don't believe you do. She's not frank and open, as a good woman ought to be, and that's just what brought me here. She came up to relieve me a few minutes ago, and called me into the little conservatory on the second floor. 'Miss Martin,' she said—and she was nervous, too, you could see that—'Miss Martin, I am going to ask you to do me a great favor. My brother, Mr. Ellis, is here. He has been unfortunate—politics, which you and I don't understand, Miss Martin—and I have offered him a home here for a time. But my husband and my brother have had an unfortunate difference of opinion and I hope you will see the inadvisability of letting Mr. St. John know that Mr. Ellis is here. May I ask your promise?'"

"Did you promise?"

"I did, like a fool. When a woman with big baby-blue eyes and a tear in each corner of them asks you to do something, you do it. But it goes against my grain to see people living on the hospitality of a dying man and deceiving him. And coming on top of what happened in the train, I don't like it, doctor."

"We must be careful to remember one thing, Miss Martin," I said as she went toward the door. "We are here to look after Mr. St. John's welfare, physical and mental. We are not responsible for his family in any way, and if it pleases them to keep from him the knowledge of a fact that it would annoy him to be told, our only course is to assist in saving him from any such annoyance. As for Miss Ellis, that little incident in the car could probably be easily explained."

Miss Martin was much older than I, and in my cub days at the hospital had even patronized me somewhat. There was something painfully reminiscent of those days of my inexperience in her next remark.

"Give a girl a straight nose and hair that waves without curlers," she said, "and she can commit murder and arson, and explain it!"

She slammed the door behind her, and left me alone and a little angry. She was right—that was the worst of it. It was only about seven hours since I first saw Georgia Ellis and she had been openly unfriendly during most of that period. Yet already I could not conceive of her in an unworthy situation. I found myself hunting excuses, explanations, and I knew that I preferred veiled hostility from her to open friendliness from any other woman. Franklin used to say that such things happened only in the twenties, and I was just enough below thirty to come under his rule.

It was no use settling down to read again. I thought over the whole thing, point by point, and evolved nothing. One thing impressed me, however; Mr. St. John had not told me of the midnight visitor on the car. That he had a reason was evident, but I could not fathom it and at last I gave it up and went to my rooms. There, until time to dress for dinner, I pored over my books, for I had a theory of my own about my patient's condition and was working it out carefully. I read a while, wrote a letter to Dr. Jamieson and dressed.

On my way downstairs I dropped the letter in the post-bag, which hung in a rear hallway.

Then, seeing no one about, I sauntered into the library and nosed around among the books. Dinner was announced to me there and I found Georgia Ellis waiting in the dining-room.

"We are to dine together," she said almost cordially. "Mrs. St. John has a headache, and her brother is away from home."

"I am sorry for the headache," I said, "but glad we are to dine together. I haven't dined for ages."

"You must be famishing." She smiled in the friendliest way in the world.

"Well, not that," I said; "what I meant to say was that at the hospital we didn't dine—we supped in the evening; you know," indefinitely—"canned salmon, prunes, crackers and fried potatoes!"

"How awful!" she said sympathetically, "and you don't appear ill-nourished, either."

"Oh there was a dinner, of a sort," I amended. "We had it at noon, you see; lots of stewed chicken—out of the broth for patients, you know—and watery custards for dessert."

I was entirely in earnest, although I believe she thought it at least in part a jest. But the meal was cozy beyond belief, my vis-a-vis was what her appearance had told me she could be if she wished, a very charming and cultured girl, clever and animated, with a pretty wit of her own. I did not afterward remember what I ate, but I did remember every flash of her eyes, every gesture of her splendidly poised head.

After dinner, however, I was doomed to disappointment. She went at once to Mrs. St. John and I made an evening visit to my patient. Afterward I went to the library and gathered an armful of books to take to my den, stopping at the mail-bag to get my letter to Dr. Jamieson. I had decided to wait a day or so, and clear up a few minor symptoms before writing. The mail-bag was where I found it before, but my letter was gone!

I could not grasp it for a moment. I felt around the inside of the bag, but met only emptiness. Then I called the butler.

"Saunders," I said, "when was the mail taken down to the village?"

"It doesn't go until morning, sir. One of the grooms takes the mail-bag down at eight o'clock."

I did not consider it advisable to mention the missing letter, but I found myself face to face with another puzzling incident and, as before, it involved Georgia Ellis. With Mrs. St. John ill and her brother away, who else in the house could have the faintest interest in my correspondence? What interest, in fact, had she?

I gave up all idea of reading then, and went thoughtfully out into the cool and quiet of the veranda. Somehow the mystery that seemed ripe in that big house seemed to stifle me. I wanted darkness and solitude to think things over.

It was cool, but not frosty. The air was full of the chirping and singing of crickets and tree-frogs, and bats were circling and darting through the trees. I wandered idly over to the stone bridge and stood there, looking at the starlight reflected from the water below. I leaned over the parapet, fragrant with nasturtiums, and tried to marshal into order the events of the last twenty-four hours—the midnight visitor to the car; the strange actions of Georgia Ellis in the stateroom; the conspiracy to keep Mr. St. John in ignorance of his brother-in-law's presence, and, last, my missing letter.

Then, without any warning whatever, the stillness of the night was broken by a wild cry, a shriek which seemed the essence of terror, and which trailed off into an inarticulate groan. For one awful minute I stood still, while a chill of pure nervous fright shook me. Then I started to run toward the house.

The lower room was brilliantly lighted and, far over, in Mr. St. John's wing, there was a dim illumination. The rest of the building was almost dark, but suddenly a light flashed up in the tower room over mine and for an instant I had a glimpse of a woman's face.

CHAPTER FOUR

The light disappeared almost immediately, as if a shade had been drawn or a shutter clapped to. As I got near the house I heard footsteps coming rapidly from the rear, and at the corner of the front veranda I almost ran into Saunders, the butler. In the light from the library window I could see his face, and it was drawn and white with terror.

"What was it, doctor?" he gasped, steadying himself against the rail of the porch. I was almost equally excited.

"I don't know," I said, "but I'm going in to find out. It seemed to come from the upper part of the house. Do any of the servants sleep there?"

"No, none, sir. We all have our quarters in a rear building—the green shingle house by the stable. Besides, all the house people are there now; we've been playing cards in the house-keeper's room."

Out of the darkness another man emerged, only partly dressed and struggling into his coat as he ran. I recognized him as one of the stablemen.

"Good Lord, what was that noise?" he asked, trying to button his coat with fingers that shook violently. "It woke me out of a sound sleep. Is the master worse, doctor?"

"It didn't come from Mr. St. John's apartments," I said positively. "Saunders, you come with me, and you"—to the other man—"watch the staircases, front and rear, that no one comes down. here's some mischief doing, but I don't know where."

Saunders followed me quietly up the stairs. First I went to the west wing and tiptoed into Mr. St. John's bedroom. The light was burning dimly and the sick man was asleep, his thin hands under his head, his lips slightly parted.

At the window Miss Martin was peering out, and she turned with a start when we entered the room. She glanced from me to Saunders, who stood in the doorway, and motioned to us not to rouse the sleeping man. Then she led the way into the adjoining dressing-room and closed the door.

"It wasn't a dream then?" she said. "There's been murder done, doctor!"

"I can't wait to talk about it." I was excited and a bit rough probably. "If things are all right here I am going to search the rest of the house."

"Just a minute." She looked at Saunders and I asked him to step into the hall. "Someone has been at my medicines again, doctor—and I'm going home tomorrow. I can't stand the strain."

"Nonsense," I said angrily, "you're too sensible for hysteria, Miss Martin, so for heaven's sake brace up; I may need you."

I left her then and hurried into the hall. We went rapidly along the corridor, past suites of guestrooms, all empty and dark, to Mrs. St. John's apartments. Here the door was open and lights burned dimly, but the rooms were empty. I was not surprised at this, for I was confident that the face at the upper tower window had been that of the mistress of the house. At the door to Miss Ellis's dressing room, which was closed, I knocked and, receiving no answer, tried the knob. It was locked!

I felt a sudden sinking of fear. What was beyond in that quiet room? Was it from there had come that awful cry, which meant agony, perhaps death? I put my shoulder against the door, and it gave slightly.

"Here, Saunders," I panted, "put your knee against the lower panel. Now!"

"What in the world are you doing, doctor?" said a quiet voice behind me. I stopped suddenly and turned around. Behind me in the dim light of the corridor was Georgia Ellis, very calm and composed, with a slightly amused smile on her lips, and her eyes wide and puzzled.

"Thank God," I said, "it isn't you, anyhow!"

"But it is I," she smiled. "Do I look like a ghost? And why all these heroics?"

"There was a shriek," I said stupidly, "a cry, and I feared some terrible accident. It is strange you did not hear it. It alarmed even the stablemen."

"Don't you think the unusual quiet has got on your nerves, doctor? I have excellent ears, and I heard nothing alarming. That is, I did hear the cry of a mountain lion, but I paid little attention. There has been one around, the natives say, for years."

Saunders looked relieved.

"That must have been what we heard, doctor," he said—"sort of soft at first, miss, and getting louder?"

"Precisely," she said, with a smile that dazzled poor Saunders. "Are you reassured, doctor?"

"Mrs. St. John?" I asked, still obstinately unconvinced.

"Is sleeping in my room. She sometimes does when she is not well," she said promptly.

"And her brother?"

"Is away from home."

"Just one more question," I said apologetically, "I don't want to be a nuisance, but where are the stairs to the upper floor?"

Perhaps I imagined it, but for just a moment I fancied she paled. Yet her voice was unembarrassed when she answered me.

"Certainly you may know," she said. "There are two shut-in staircases, but as the rooms up there are never used, the doors to the stairways are kept locked and Mr. St. John has the keys someplace."

I was beaten, baffled, but unconvinced. Just then Saunders uttered a quick exclamation and pointed to the girl's hand. She looked, too, and held it up, with a dismayed face. It was covered with bright red blood, and the lace of her loose white sleeve was crimson.

"Mercy," she said, "I had no idea it was bleeding! It's only a scratch, for all the show it makes; I cut my arm a trifle with a brass paper-knife a few minutes ago."

"Let me attend to it for you," I said eagerly. "It ought to be washed and bandaged, you know. A brass paper-knife can make a nasty cut."

"Nonsense," she said sharply, moving toward the door of her room. "I tell you it is only a scratch, and I won't be bothered with a bandage. I am going to bed, and if you are wise you will give up hunting for uncanny things and do the same."

She took a key from the pocket of her loose white negligee, slipped it into the lock, opened the door and was gone, with a curt good night. As the door closed softly behind her, I heard the unmistakable slipping of a bolt, and I stood in the hall looking at the shining panels I had tried to force.

Saunders was much relieved. He went downstairs, and I could hear him talking to the stableman we had left on guard. Then the front doors closed and the house was quiet.

I went back to my den and sat down at the square weathered-oak table, with its shaded lamp, and went over the events of the last half-hour.

Of one thing I was convinced. Reasonably or unreasonably, I felt in my heart that Georgia Ellis had not cut her arm; that somewhere, probably in the tower room just over my head, had been at least the beginning of tragedy. And another thing: if Mrs. St. John was sleeping in her cousin's bedroom, why should that cousin lock the door and take the key with her?

The tree-toads and crickets were still singing their melancholy and monotonous songs, a frog croaked hoarsely down by the stone bridge, and over in his quiet room the owner of all this big house slept on, in ignorance of the tragedy that seemed in the very air.

CHAPTER FIVE

Georgia—I called her Georgia to myself already—and I breakfasted alone. She was rather quiet and ate little, and I thought
she watched me with troubled, childish eyes. She was very
young, this girl, and very lovely; not for a moment did I connect
her with crime, except as a victim or an unwilling accomplice,
and as I sat opposite her and noted, as she poured out my coffee,
the bit of plaster on her wrist, I was ashamed of my previous
night's suspicions.

"My cousin always breakfasts in her room," she said simply,
"but after this morning you will not be so lonely. Mr. St. John's
uncle telegraphed that he would arrive at noon, and I am sure
you will like him. He is a dear old fellow, a widower for many
years, with always some sort of fad to keep him company,
instead of a wife."

"That's a very empty existence," I said. "A fad is a very poor
substitute for a pleasant face across the breakfast table and
someone to pour out one's coffee."

She laughed a little, but not self-consciously. "How is your
wrist?" I asked.

"Oh, I forget it until I see the plaster." She held up a slim white
hand. "It was a trifle, you know. I am afraid I was rude about it

last night, but it seemed absurd to wash and bandage so small a cut."

"It bled a lot," I said, looking directly into her eyes. "It must have struck a blood vessel."

For one electrifying moment I thought she was going to tell me everything. We were quite alone; Saunders had gone out to his pantry.

"Dr. Pierce"—she leaned toward me on the table—"I want to tell you—I feel—"

Saunders came in again, and the impulse, whatever it was, was succeeded by caution. Not again, for many days, did she proffer me a confidence, and then only when it was forced from her.

Directly after breakfast I went to my patient's room. Jones, his valet, was shaving him, and I was appalled to see how worn he looked in the clear morning light. In the next room Miss Martin was breakfasting, served by one of the housemaids. She got up when I entered, but I motioned her to go on and drew my chair to her small table. The housemaid put on the rest of the breakfast and withdrew.

Miss Martin was a creature of physical, rather than mental, characteristics, and her emotions were largely influenced by her meals. She was a pessimist before dinner, an optimist after. So now with the remains of an excellent cantaloupe on the side table, and with a delicious breakfast and a little silver pot of coffee before her, she was inclined to make light of her previous evening's suspicions.

"I may have been mistaken, doctor, about the medicines," she said. "I was wakened suddenly by that noise—it was a mountain lion, Jane tells me—and I thought some of my bottles had been disturbed. But I'm not at all certain. In fact, I think I was mistaken."

"Who was in the room during the evening?"

"Only Mrs. St. John. She had a headache, she said, and stayed only a few minutes."

"Are you there. Pierce?" called St. John from the next room, and I went in.

Jones and Miss Martin had got him out of bed, and he was lying on a couch in the big window, looking at the tangle of forest trees and thickets outside. There had been a slight frost, and the leaves in that one night's foretaste of winter had put on their warmer reds and yellows. There was an open wood fire crackling in the grate, and a big bunch of chrysanthemums, ripened with the first touch of cold, glowed on a table.

For various reasons I dreaded the interview. He had a peculiar faculty of jumping to conclusions, not by what was said, but rather by what was not said—a faculty of intuition sometimes developed abnormally in people who must rely on others for their knowledge of affairs and persons.

I knew that in some way I must conceal from him the fact that anything unusual had happened. To tell him of the cry, the light in the tower room, the blood, would be to put him in a dangerously excited condition. All that I could hope was to keep him in ignorance until I had found a solution of the mystery; then I could decide as to the advisability of telling him all—or nothing.

"Sit down, Pierce," he said. "I have told Miss Martin to take a walk for an hour. She looks rather seedy this morning, and anyhow I wanted to see you alone. Is there anything new? Have you found anything out of the ordinary?"

"Well, it's a little soon," I said evasively. "Things have been very quiet and I haven't seen Mrs. St. John since yesterday at luncheon. She has not been well."

"She is far from well," he said emphatically. "She came to see how I slept, and her face was ghastly. I wish you would talk to her, Pierce. She may need some medicine."

"I will," I agreed. It was not necessary to tell him that I had offered to make up something for her headache and had been refused. "If she is better we are going to play bridge this evening after you are ready to go to sleep, and I will watch her closely then. So far I have observed nothing but a capricious appetite, and this headache, of course."

We were silent for a few minutes. St. John lay quiet, watching a squirrel on the branch of a tree near his window. Pretty soon the little fellow gave a jump and landed on the window sill. I noticed then that outside the window the ledge had been sprinkled with nuts. St. John drew a long breath and turned to me.

"It's harder, Pierce," he said slowly, "I thought in the hospital that it would be easier if I could get up here to Laurelcrest again, and see the squirrels, and watch the sun go down over the mountains a few times, I'd be ready to go. But I can't give it up. Pierce. I'm afraid I'm going to fight it."

I had a choking kind of lump in my throat. I'm rather callous as a rule—hospital work is hardening. But here was a man not much older than I, with an intellect unclouded by disease, and with no suffering to make the end a relief, and he was dying by inches!

"We spent our honeymoon here," he went on. "It was late spring and the rose garden was full of roses. I remember when we got here how fragrant everything was with them. The housekeeper was an old family servant and she had put pink bride-roses everywhere. It was here, too, last spring that I got a fall from my horse. I have always given my wife the impression that my trouble is an injury of the leg dating from that time."

"I have never heard the particulars," I said. "I knew through the papers that you were hurt."

"There are no sensational details. My horse bolted, and then, going at top speed, caught his foot and fell. He kicked me twice, once on the leg and once on the head. There was no fracture in any place, and in a couple of weeks I was about again, apparently all right. But in a month or so the toe of that foot began to drag, and you know the rest. The periods of unconsciousness seem to me to be closer together and to last longer in the last month, but I don't think Jamieson is right about his diagnosis. His prognosis is good—or bad—enough, but I don't believe it is Jacksonian or any other kind of epilepsy. I've been reading up about it, you see." He pointed to some books piled on a table, and I examined them curiously.

"I've given Jamieson a fair trial," he went on. "I think he has done the best he can, but he won't listen to any opinion but his own, and since he has given me up I think I am justified in trying someone else. I've been thinking, Pierce, of putting the matter into your hands, and asking you to bring up one of the younger men, one a little more progressive than Jamieson. These older men don't give me a ghost of a chance; now let's see what a younger man can do."

I was staggered for a moment. I had been glad to come up to Laurelcrest, as substitute and largely under the direction of Jamieson, but I was not prepared to have the entire responsibility thrust on me. It was gratifying, as well as astounding.

"If you are not afraid to try me," I said, "I'll do the best I can."

"For instance," he went on, pursuing a train of thought that he had evidently considered before, "we might start with the hypothesis that it is not epileptic, and not incurable. Then work from that."

"I have already considered that possibility," I said, with due modesty. "In fact, I wrote something of the kind to Jamieson last night, but . . ."

"But what?" he asked, with quick suspicion. "The letter is gone," I finished lamely.

"Well, telegraph to him that I am making a change in treatment. That ought to be sufficient. And now, Mr. Physician-in-charge, what is our next move?"

"Our next move, I think, will be to send for Carter," I said thoughtfully. "He's one of the new men, an aggressive kind of fellow who doesn't know the word conservatism, and who isn't hampered by precedent."

"The very thing," said St. John. "By all means send for Carter."

I wrote a telegram while he watched me, his eyes with a new sparkle of hope in them, his sunken cheeks flushed, and rose to make arrangements for sending it. He called me back from the door to whisper that his wife must know nothing of it—it would alarm her unnecessarily. Couldn't Carter come at night? So I rewrote the message and went out as Miss Martin came in.

I found Georgia Ellis in the hall, hatted and ulstered, with a pair of loose driving-gloves in her hand.

"I'm going for Uncle Hotchkiss," she said gaily. "You may come, too, if you'll sit in the rumble coming back."

I would have walked back cheerfully for the pleasure of driving down with her to the village, nd said so. I have an idea that all the men she knew said the same things, and meant them, too. But if the homage was not new, it was at least not unpleasing.

"Hurry," she called after me. "We must not be late for the train."

The horse was fresh, the air crisp and bracing, and the drive long to be remembered.

Georgia was an experienced whip, daring to recklessness, and we jolted over ruts and bounced over rocks in a perfect delirium of speed. It was much too rapid for me; my idea of a drive with the girl beside me was a careful and deliberate proceeding, averaging four or five miles an hour, and a good deal of conversation.

Such conversation as we did was mainly staccato, punctuated with harrowing periods when we swung around a corner on two wheels.

Once we spied a man on the road before us. He was swinging along with easy strides, and at first I did not recognize him. We overtook and passed him at breakneck speed, but he lifted his hat and waved it after us, and I saw it was Frank Ellis.

All too soon we were in the outskirts of the little town, and Georgia was pointing out places of interest with the butt of her whip.

"The rectory," she said, indicating a small white building. "Six children and four hundred dollars a year—until Harry St. John doubled it. The red brick is the church, and the janitor lives in that shanty at the back of it. He gets a dollar and a half a week, and is allowed to pasture his cow in the graveyard."

Her gaiety was contagious. All trace of the previous day's hostility was gone; she was effervescing with the joy of living, and I felt that I was seeing the natural side of her character. More than ever I was convinced that she was helping to bear another's burden, and that, temporarily at least, the weight had been lifted.

We drew up at the station with a flourish, and I climbed down and threaded my way among mud-spattered buggies and spring-wagons to the yellow-frame building. At the ticket office a young woman left the telegraph instrument long enough to tell me that the train was late, indefinitely late. Two hours it might be, possibly four; a washout had caused a wreck and the line was blocked.

I reported this to Georgia, and she was less dismayed than I had expected.

"It will be rather a lark," she said. "There's no use risking our necks and the springs of the trap by going back to Laurelcrest for luncheon. We can drive about, and when we get hungry there's a place here called the 'Farmer's Haven' where we can get something to eat. It's the kind of place, you know, where somebody— I forget who—says they serve canned corn in birds' bathtubs, and they have a pitcher of buttermilk on the table."

"The idea is an inspiration," I said. "I adore canned corn, and I prefer buttermilk to champagne—under certain circumstances."

"Do you know," she said quizzically, "I begin to think you did not always live in a hospital."

"Once, sweet lady, I had a home," I began melodramatically. "Which reminds me, Miss Ellis, that some day I want to tell you about my father. He's—well, I think you will be interested."

"I am sure of it," she said heartily. "And now, where?"

"I have a telegram to send," I recollected suddenly, "If you will take a prescription to the drugstore—I'm told there's a pharmacy of a sort—while I send my message, we shall be ready to drive in ten minutes."

I wrote a prescription for a tonic for Mr. St. John and gave it to her. She turned the horse cleverly, and I watched her down the dusty street; then I went in and sent my message to Carter.

Important case, can you come to Carson, via P. & L., on train arriving
at 9 p.m.? Will meet you. Answer at once. Pierce.

I sent it to the college where Carter lectured on surgery, and counted on an answer before we left for Laurelcrest. By the time the message was off Georgia Ellis was coming up the street again, and in a few minutes we were out of the settlement and flying along a level road.

I don't remember what we talked about on that memorable occasion, but I do remember exactly how the hair grew in a soft curve around the tops of her ears, and that she had a dimple in the center of her chin, I still recall the thrill I felt when the ends of her loose chiffon veil flapped in my face, and how, when Ned pulled pretty hard and her gloves bothered her, she stripped them off, and I put them, still warm, into my pocket. I have an idea that we talked much about myself—my hopes and plans, the postponed trip to Germany, my desire to study a specialty, and from that, quite naturally, to Carter, although of course I did not mention his approaching visit.

"He's a big fellow," I said enthusiastically, "very broad-shouldered and muscular, with dark eyes and heavy black hair, and the younger men fairly set him on a pedestal."

"Does he resemble you?" she asked.

"You are a big fellow, with dark eyes and heavy black hair." I laughed at the idea.

"Not even faintly," I confessed. "Why, Carter's an Adonis, with very regular features—almost classical—and—"

"I dislike perfect features in a man," she said decidedly. And for some reason I felt comforted.

The meal at the "Farmer's Haven" was a delight. We had very thin steak, fried hard, and at least a dozen, between us, of little oval vegetable dishes, each containing a modicum of stewed vegetable. Then we had pie, real country-hotel pie, which, in a region where berries are plenty and cheap, puts in just enough fruit to keep the two layers of crust from sticking together. It was a delightful meal, and lasted longer than we knew.

When we got back to the station the belated train had arrived. A little thin man, with grayish hair and nervous, near-sighted eyes, was on the platform. Georgia threw me the reins and climbed down, and a moment later she was shaking hands with "Uncle Hotchkiss." He greeted her cordially, but I noticed an air of abstraction as they came toward us. Then, almost at the trap, he broke away from her and disappeared in the crowd.

"Isn't that exactly like him!" The girl was both vexed and amused. "He's the most unreliable and altogether likable old man I ever knew. There's nothing to do now but wait for him."

"I'm expecting an answer to my message," I said, as I helped her in. "Suppose I try to coax him back in this direction?"

"The very thing," she assented.

My message from Carter was laconic to the point of slang. It was the one word "Sure" and his initials. Then I hunted out Mr. Hotchkiss.

He was standing in close conversation with a stout, middle-aged country-woman, whose heavy features bore signs of recent tears.

"It ought not to be difficult," he said. "I sat directly behind you and distinctly saw you pay your fare and put your purse back in your pocket. You find your purse gone and your pocket cut out of your gown, so I am telling you how it happened, and how the police can find the man; I have it written down."

"You saw him? Why didn't you stop him?" asked the woman suspiciously.

"I did not see him do it," went on Mr. Hotchkiss mildly, "but after he left the car I saw your pocket on the ground. Allow me."

He produced from his pocket a black alpaca pocket, which had been neatly severed from its surroundings, and gave it to the woman. She took it, her jaw dropping with amazement and her face flushed with anger.

"You did it yourself!" she shrieked. "You can't fool me with your high and mighty airs. You've got my purse now!"

"And here, madam," he persisted, still gravely courteous, "is a card on which you will find a description of the man, the make of his watch and the manufacturer's name in his overcoat, and the stations where he entered and left the train."

The woman set her jaw with sudden determination. "Sam!" she called to a hulking fellow in a muddy spring wagon. I saw there was no time to waste and did not wait to introduce myself.

As the man in the spring wagon wrapped his reins about the whip, preparatory to dismounting, I took Mr. Hotchkiss by the arm and pulled him toward the trap.

"It's a misunderstanding." I explained, as we hurried along. "She thinks you have her purse, and no amount of explaining would clear things up. Here you are, sir."

We drove out of town as rapidly as we had come in. From my seat in the rumble I could watch the mystified faces on the station platform gradually fade into a safe obscurity. Mr. Hotchkiss was rather gloomy, and after a lengthy dissertation on the obtuseness to modem detective methods shown by people in rural districts, he lapsed into silence.

"It is one of his hobbies to fancy himself a great amateur detective," Georgia whispered to me, when the little man had disappeared into the house and we waited together for a groom. "He follows all the criminal cases in the papers, and some of his deductions are really wonderful."

I smiled, with the tolerance of youth for the hobbies of middle-age. I was more interested in Georgia Ellis than in the man she was talking of. But later, when trouble had come thick and heavy, I was glad to remember her words.

Dinner that night was the most cheerful meal since our arrival. Mrs. St. John, whose headache had disappeared, was less constrained and depressed than I had ever seen her, and Georgia Ellis was still in her gay mood of the afternoon. But perhaps the most astonishing change was in Frank Ellis. His face, which I had seen only in melancholy repose, was animated and alert; he showed himself a clever talker, with a touch of cynicism that was not ill-natured. I was prepared to dislike him, and instead found myself drawn to him. Every now and then I come across someone whom according to every precedent I should despise and dismiss, and whom I do cordially dislike—in his or her absence, only to be won over at our meeting by a sort of personal magnetism that is irresistible. It was precisely that way with Ellis.

We arranged to go out over the mountains the next morning, and were debating the route, helped by suggestions from Georgia and Mrs. St. John, when I heard Miss Martin's excited voice in the hall. I excused myself and hurried out, to find the nurse, white and trembling, just outside the door.

"Oh, doctor, I'm afraid it's too late!" She began to cry then, and without waiting to hear more I started to run up the stairs. She followed me, and I could catch a word here and there. It was something about "capsules" and "unconscious"; but the word that rang in my ears as I flew along the upper hall was "poison"!

CHAPTER SEVEN

The sick room was bright with lamps, as if Miss Martin had suddenly realized that things were not right and had hastily examined her patient in a better light. On the bed, his eyes not entirely closed, his face slightly suffused, lay Harry St. John.

His skin was warm and moist as I felt his pulse—what pulse there was, for its beats, like his respirations, were slow and irregular, with painfully long intervals between. I scarcely knew my own voice when I told Miss Martin to bring a light close, and her hands were shaking so that the flame of the lamp flickered and wavered. But it was the man's eyes that told the story; the pupils were contracted and insensitive to light, and the small vessels were suffused and swollen. The symptoms, the unconsciousness, suffused skin, slow breathing and contracted pupils pointed clearly to an overwhelming dose of a narcotic poison, opium or its alkaloid—morphia, probably.

There was no time even to conjecture how he had got the stuff. Action, quick, decisive action, was necessary if we would save our patient. In a dozen words I had got Miss Martin to work, and with something to do she braced up again and became her usual resourceful self.

"Get me some atropine," I said, "and ring for ice and strong black coffee. Where's your hypodermic?"

I had not noticed the presence of Mrs. St. John, but now I saw her on her knees beside the bed, one of the unconscious man's hands held to her cheek, her eyes wild and despairing. For a moment I resented her presence; somehow I felt that in an indirect way—some way which I could not fathom—the mystery which existed in the house, and with which she was in some way connected, was responsible for this new development. Then I saw Georgia Ellis in the doorway. She was as white as the dinner dress she wore, and she was steadying herself with one hand against the doorway.

"What is it?" she asked, "Has he fainted? I thought Miss Martin—said . . ."

"She did," I said brutally, "and I'm afraid she is right. It is poison of some sort, probably morphia. Get me some alcohol, Miss Martin."

As I glanced up from filling the hypodermic I saw Georgia put her hand to her throat, look with horrified eyes at the quiet figure on the bed and walk unsteadily away. Mrs. St. John's face was gray, her lips colorless, as she got to her feet and faced me across the bed.

"Do you mean that he has been poisoned? That—that he is dying?" She was making a terrible effort to keep her senses. "Tell me it isn't so, doctor! It cannot be! It cannot be!"

"We must not give up hope," I said more gently. "We have found it out early, which is anadvantage. But we are going to have a struggle, and I think you would better wait in the hall. Get a chair and sit there, and you can help by sending for the things we need."

She went, blindly groping her way to the door, a pitiful figure whose costly gown only enhanced the lifeless gray of her face.

At the door she turned, looked long at the man on the bed, and went out.

A moment later the door opened to admit Ells. He had a bowl of black coffee in his hand, and he set it down and came over to the bed.

"Can I do anything?" he asked. "I studied medicine for a couple of years, and I can fetch and carry things for you, anyhow. What do you think it is?"

"Morphia, probably," I said, "and I'll be glad to have your help. Fix up a basin of ice water and slap his back with a towel dipped in it."

He worked quietly and systematically, doing what he was told, and no more. I was glad to have him, glad to have anyone with a little technical training, to talk to. A groom had already started to Carson with a request to the only doctor in the neighborhood to come up and to bring some permanganate. But it would be two hours at best before assistance came and in the interval we worked feverishly.

After an hour or so there was a slight improvement. Pulse and respiration were better, the patient appeared to resent his vigorous pounding with the water, and his eyes began to look more normal. At last we stopped for a few minutes rest, and I opened the door into the hall. Georgia was there alone, pacing anxiously backward and forward, her hands clenched nervously together.

"How is he?" she asked, as I stepped out and closed the door behind me. "Rousing a little. He's in pretty fair shape now, if his heart lasts."

"Thank God!" she said fervently. "Will you tell Frank I want to see him, doctor?"

I sent him out, not without a pang of jealousy, and took his place by the bed. Miss Martin was looking worn and tired, with dark lines under her eyes and little drawn lines at the corners of her mouth. I had time now to wonder how and when the poison had been administered and we discussed the affair with carefully lowered voices.

"What medicines have you given him today?" I asked.

"He has had only the medicines we brought from the hospital and the gelatine capsules you brought from the village."

"Could anyone have entered the room while you were absent?"

"I think not, doctor. Jones was here once or twice, but he could not have given him anything that I did not see."

"It might have been in his food," I reflected. "That is sent from the kitchen, isn't it?"

"Not tonight," she said decisively. "He was not hungry and I prepared some clam bouillon myself. After that he took the tonic and prepared for sleep."

The sick man stirred and mumbled inarticulately, then lapsed again into sleep. "Let me see the capsules," I said suddenly.

She brought me a small box, a pink affair without a label, and held it out to me, I took one of the bullet-shaped gelatine cases and pulled it apart. The powder which it contained fell on my hand in a tiny white heap. I touched it to my tongue, and the bitterness was conclusive.

"We shall not have to look further, Miss Martin," I said. "This is not the medicine I ordered. The capsules I prescribed were larger, and the medicine brown. It is an error at the pharmacy."

I drew a long breath of relief. So it was not a dastardly attempt at murder after all. The emotion of the two women had been the natural result of the shock, uncoupled with guilt.

"Did you see the man put up the medicine, doctor?"

The question was innocent, the nurse's voice hinted at a

deeper meaning. If I had not—and someone else had! Good heavens, and Georgia Ellis had attended to the prescription and given me the box at the door downstairs!

"It is an error in filling out the prescription, beyond a doubt," I said, evasively, "and we can only be thankful that it is turning out so well."

When the elderly man from the village bustled in, Ellis took me to one side.

"I'm going now," he said. "I'm not needed any longer, and I believe you know I'm a sort of *persona non grata* around here."

"You've been a lot of help," I assured him. "You've given up your medical studies for good?"

"Yes," he assented gloomily. "There are—reasons."

Dr. Millard stayed until morning. As the drug wore off we did all we could to attract the sick man's wandering attention; we asked him questions and tried to make him answer; we attempted to argue—he begged to be allowed to sleep; we attacked his politics, even his religion—only to have him slip back again into stupor. Toward morning I was desperate, and Miss Martin came forward with a suggestion.

"Ask him about the tray of medicines in the car," she said.

I tried it. Dr. Millard had dozed off in his chair, and was snoring loudly. I leaned over and made another attempt to rouse St. John.

"About your wife," I suggested. "Was it Mrs. St. John?" He roused a trifle.

"Was it Mrs. St. John who took the medicine from the tray in the stateroom?"

He seemed to puzzle over the question, and I repeated it. Then we had the first reward for our night's work.

"No—Georgia," he said thickly, and I knew the battle was won.

As the first bluish shadows of early dawn touched the tops of the mountains, I sent for his wife and she came slowly in, still in the pink gown of the evening before. He knew her, and smiled faintly as she knelt beside him; and so they stayed, while the sun came into the valley, and the birds began to sing.

CHAPTER EIGHT

By noon that day things were moving along in their accustomed channels. To St. John we explained what had happened as the result of a drug clerk's error, and if he suspected that I was not entirely frank, he at least said nothing.

"Let me see the capsules," he said, when I had finished. I went to the table and looked around for the box. It was not there. Miss Martin came and we searched together, but the box was gone, and in its place on the medicine tray was a small yellow box, duly labeled by the Carson pharmacy, and containing round, flat cases filled with brownish powder.

Miss Martin's eyes met mine with a horrified gaze. For a minute I stood stupidly staring; then the need of dissimulation roused me.

"Here they are," I said, taking the box over to the bed. "They don't look deadly, do they?" He turned one of the capsules over in his hand curiously.

"Take care of them. Pierce," he said, as he put it back in the box. The next time there may not be any pharmacy clerk around to blame it on."

Whatever he meant, he did not pursue the subject further, and I was glad to change the conversation.

"Carter will be here tonight," I said. "I am going to Carson to meet the nine o'clock train."

"You are sure Mrs. St. John knows nothing of it?"

"Positive."

"I've lost my nerve," he confessed. "Whether it's because I'm sore all over from the beating you gave me last night, or whatever the reason is, I wish you wouldn't leave me. Pierce. Send Uncle Hotchkiss down to the train; he is discretion itself, and he can make his eccentricity a reason for taking out a cart at that hour of the night. Then you can smuggle Dr. Carter into the house easily—there's a side entrance for this wing. I don't hope much from this visit," he said drearily, as Miss Martin left the room, "but I must take every chance to recover, if only to help my wife out of this trouble, whatever it is."

I found an opportunity that afternoon to approach Mr. Hotchkiss. He was standing in the hall, nervously buttoning up a light overcoat, and he welcomed my suggestion that I should accompany him on his stroll.

"I've been very much put out," he said, as we went down the steps of the veranda. "With the excitement in the house this morning, no one went for the papers, and it has spoiled my entire day. Have you been reading the Dawes murder case?"

I was obliged to confess I had not.

"It's a rather complicated affair," he said, "but stripped of its trimmings it is simply this: A man sues an insurance company to collect insurance on his wife, the wife having been thrown from a bridge in a runaway and drowned. The insurance company asserts that the woman was dead—murdered—before she was thrown into the water, and point to a contusion of the head. Well, sir, up to this point the crazy experts in the case have examined and pronounced on her stomach, lungs, heart and liver. Bah! And the only single decisive clue never touched!"

"Indeed," I said politely, "what is the clue?"

"You medical men are all alike," he snorted. "Once the breath of life leaves the body, and there's no more chance for ten-dollar consultations and three-dollar visits, then you're done with it. The clue, man? The middle ear, of course. There's always sand or foreign matter in the middle ear after death by drowning. And they've had that poor creature's lungs to court in a bucket."

He was perfectly in earnest, so I did not smile. Besides, he had furnished an excuse for the trip Iwas going to ask him to make that night.

"You can get the morning papers at Carson tonight," I suggested. "I have a friend coming out on the nine o'clock train, and if you are going down you might bring him back with you."

"Certainly, certainly," he assented. "Very glad to do it."

"I am bringing up another doctor to see your nephew, Mr. Hotchkiss. I am not satisfied with his condition; he's not recovering the way he should."

"He's not recovering at all," he said gruffly. "What's the matter with his wife, that she can't see it?"

"He keeps it from her. He doesn't want her to be worried."

"Fiddlesticks! She's worrying about something else then; she looks like an old woman."

I had an impulse then to tell him the whole thing. There was something in his shrewd old face, with its nervously alert but not unkindly eyes, that made me feel that he could be trusted to any extent.

"There are a good many things I don't understand, Mr. Hotchkiss. I wouldn't be at all surprised if you can find a case as interesting as the Dawes case, right here. If there hasn't been murder, there has been what looks like attempted murder."

He squared around and looked at me, his eyes blinking behind his glasses. Then he took out a little notebook and sat down beside the road.

"Go on," he said.

"I'll give it to you briefly, then we can go over and elaborate it. In the first place, early last spring, Mr. St. John was thrown from his horse and kicked. You know that. What you probably do not know is that since a month or so after that time he has been a victim of a creeping paralysis which now involves his entire right leg."

"I thought it was an injury to a joint."

"He has given that impression, especially to his wife. He dreads giving her pain—does not want her to know the hopelessness of his condition."

"Hopeless, is it? Poor Harry!" Mr. Hotchkiss wiped his glasses and coughed huskily. "Well, well, and he's only a boy."

"I am not sure that it is hopeless," I went on guardedly; "that is why I am bringing another man up tonight. You can understand that your nephew wishes his visit to be a profound secret."

He nodded. "Well?"

I told him then the strange events of the last few days; the nocturnal visitor as the car lay on the side track, the incident of Miss Ellis and the medicines in the stateroom, the request that I keep from Mr. St. John the fact that Ellis was in the house, the change in the servants, the shriek from the tower room, the incident of Miss Ellis's cut hand and, last, the disappearance of the capsules in the pink box.

He took them all down, numbered in proper order, and with exquisite neatness. Through it all he had said nothing, but he looked up now with a face from which all the boredom had fled.

"It's a very pretty muddle," he said, rubbing his hands together. "With just enough of the unusual to make it interesting. Mrs. St. John asked me to keep her brother's visit a secret, and I said I would. Political reasons—ugh! Well, I don't believe it."

He tapped his book with his pencil for a moment, looking absently at the ground. "When did Mrs. St. John hurt her arm?" he asked suddenly.

"It was Miss Ellis," I corrected.

"Oh, I know that, young man. But Mrs. St. John had a bandage on her arm under the sleeve of her gown last night."

"You saw it?" I was amazed.

"I felt it," he chuckled. "I helped her upstairs when the alarm came about Harry."

"Well, it's getting too deep for me," I admitted.

"What kind of woman is this nurse?" he asked. "Soft-voiced, ingratiating sort, afraid for her future, nurses for the love of doing good, and so on? I had one like that once."

"On the contrary, a resourceful woman of middle age, who is frankly mercenary, but very faithful."

"Um," he said thoughtfully. "Has Harry made a will?"

"I haven't the slightest idea," I said, as we started back toward the house.

"Well, it's a queer household," he said. "Here's Ellis in love with his cousin, and Mrs. St. John guarding some sort of gnawing secret. Here's Harry, the best fellow that ever lived, doomed to death by either sickness or poison, with a nurse who may or may not be an honest woman, and here, last of all, are a bit of a boy and an antediluvian fossil conspiring about something that isn't their business at all."

I flushed at that, and he patted me, reassuringly.

"Never mind," he said. "We will make it our business, you and I, and to be candid, I'm just a little flattered at your confidence. Now, you walk down to the gate tonight about ten o'clock and I'll deliver you one consultant, in good condition."

CHAPTER NINE

Dinner dragged that evening. The old air of constraint had come back again, and Mr. Hotchkiss and I did all the talking. Ellis was gloomy and silent, eating little and watching Georgia almost constantly. I thought she resented his scrutiny; once, indeed, she spoke of it, pettishly.

"What in the world is the matter, Frank? Is my hair wrong, or don't you like my gown? You make me positively uncomfortable."

"You are perfect," he said softly, and I could have knocked him down with pleasure.

Mrs. St. John sat listlessly in her chair, her color coming and going with every sound, as if she dreaded a repetition of last night's interruption. But nothing occurred. The meal ended uneventfully in the midst of a long dissertation on bats by Mr. Hotchkiss, who proved to have as many hobbies as the spinster lady of fiction has pets.

"Bats," he was saying as we made our way to the drawing-room, "are a most interesting study to the naturalist."

"People travel on them, don't they?" asked Georgia, wickedly. "I seem to have heard of people going on bats."

"You have been misinformed, my dear," said Hotchkiss

gravely, "It is a superstition, probably. I suggest that we adjourn to the veranda and study a few of their habits from life."

Anything was better than the stiff grandeur of the drawing room. As the others got wraps and prepared to go out, I ran up to St. John's room for a moment. He was awake, languidly reading by the light of a green-shaded lamp beside the bed. He had a pencil and paper beside him, and seemed to have been jotting down some sort of memoranda.

"I'm glad you came up, Pierce," he said. "I've been thinking all day that if I had—gone off last night, there would have been a lot of things not attended to. I wish you would write a note to Wheatley, of Wheatley & Johnson, and ask him to come up here. Tell him to come at once."

I wrote the letter in the little circular study which opened from his bedroom, and addressed it according to his direction.

"Let my uncle take it down tonight," he said. "I've been anxious all day to see Wheatley and straighten things out. I made a will while I was in the hospital, and I want to make some changes. For one thing, I have made no provision for my wife's brother, and although personally I dislike and distrust him, still it will be much more comfortable for Mrs. St. John if her brother has an annuity. Then another thing—I think I will double the small amount I was going to give Miss Martin. She's been more than good to me. Pierce."

"Where is she now?" I asked suddenly.

"I sent her out for a little fresh air. She hadn't been out since yesterday."

"Suppose I send the letter down and stay with you," I suggested. "I might read you to sleep."

"I've been sleeping all the afternoon," he objected, "Get Stevenson's *Treasure Island*, and read me awake, instead."

I went down to the library and got the book, then, with

the letter in my hand, went out on the veranda to find Mr. Hotchkiss. At first I thought it deserted. Down under the trees I could see Ellis and his cousin strolling together, and the dislike I always felt for the man when he was absent asserted itself again. There was no sign of Hotchkiss, but down the long drive I caught sight of a solitary figure in a cloak which I decided was Miss Martin.

I was startled by a voice from a shadowy corner of the veranda. It was Mrs. St. John, swathed in a wrap of soft white wool, and looking almost ethereally lovely in the faint light.

"Doctor," she said, as I went over to her, "I wish you would sit down and talk to me. Perhaps I imagine it, but you seem to avoid me."

"We have only just arrived," I interposed hastily, "and so many things have happened."

"Yes, it is probably morbidness on my part. I have lost my sense of proportion, doctor, things don't have their true value any more. What is it—nerves?"

"I think you are not well," I said cautiously, "and one's physical condition always influences the mental."

"No, I am not well," she confessed. "I don't sleep at all, and I'm nervous, hysterical, all the time. You won't mention it to my husband, will you? It would alarm him unnecessarily, and I am so anxious for his recovery. He is recovering, isn't he, doctor?"

"It's a little soon for the change to be of any benefit," I said evasively. "And last night, of course, was a strain."

"Last night!" she said, with a little choke in her voice. "Have you any idea how it happened—who did it, doctor? Was it a drug-clerk's error?"

"It was an error somewhere," I asserted. "We might have traced it, but the pink box that contained the capsules has disappeared."

Was it imagination, or did she draw a sigh of relief?

"I will give you a powder to make you sleep tonight," I said, as I got up. "Miss Martin will bring it to you when she comes in. I am going up now to read to Mr. St. John."

I gave the letter to Saunders and asked him to find Mr. Hotchkiss. Then I went back to the sick room. St. John was alone, staring moodily at the green shade of the lamp, and I noticed that there were new lines of bitterness around his mouth and that his dark hair seemed quite suddenly to have grayed around the temples.

I looked for the chart the nurse kept, on which she recorded all the symptoms and medicines.

It was not in the sick room or the dressing room beyond, and at last I appealed to St. John himself.

"Where does Miss Martin keep your chart?" I asked. "I want to show it to Carter when he comes."

"In her own room, I fancy," he answered. "She found Jones reading it this morning and took it away."

Miss Martin's room was back along a cross corridor. I knocked at the door, which was partly ajar, and, receiving no answer, walked in. The symptom chart was on the toilet table, and just under it lay the missing pink box, empty! For a second I was dazed. The new train of possibilities this opened in connection with the legacy St. John had mentioned flashed through my mind in a riot of conjecture. Then I put the chart down and went softly back to the sick room.

When Miss Martin came in, looking fresh and ruddy from her walk, we were deep in *Treasure Island*. I gave her the book and she took my place while I went down the side staircase and into the open air. It was almost ten when I reached the gate; it was exactly ten when Nelly, the bay mare, stopped beside me, and I recognized the towering form of Carter in the runabout.

"Ha, the plot thickens," he said in a stage whisper, as he

jumped out and shook hands with me. "What in thunder do you mean by bringing me here at this hour, no food, no bed, no drink, no anything?"

"Great Scott, haven't you had anything to eat?"

"At noon I had four oranges, a peach and a box of caramels, from the train boy. Nothing since."

There was tragedy in Carter's tone.

"I was expecting at least the usual hospitality when I arrived," he said aggrievedly. "Now I learn I am to take refuge at a hostelry called 'The Farmer's Haven'!"

I had many occasions afterward to recognize the resourcefulness of Mr. Hotchkiss, but never more than now.

"I have a suggestion, gentlemen," he said, as he hopped nimbly to the ground and fumbled nervously with the hitching strap. "I'll tie Nelly here and do a little foraging around the pantry. I can probably find a bottle of claret and something to eat. Then, Pierce, you can drive your friend to the hotel and he can eat his luncheon on the way. I'll put something in a basket under the seat, and don't forget to keep the lamps covered for a couple of hundred yards or so."

"Who is he?" asked Carter curiously as we started quietly along the hedge toward the side entrance in the west wing. "All the way up he's been asking me crazy questions—wanted to know if a blunt weapon ever made an incised wound, and if it was possible under any circumstances for a man to shoot himself in the back!"

I smiled in the darkness, but the dark, shadowy house loomed before us, and there was no chance to answer. I motioned Carter to wait, and went in the small side door and up the stairs. Everything was quiet. I could hear Miss Martin's voice, nasally monotonous, reading those inspiring adventures on Treasure Island, without an inflection, and, satisfied that everything was safe, I led Carter up to the sick room.

The next hour was given over to a thorough and exhaustive examination of the patient. At the end of that time Carter straightened and drew a long breath.

"I want you to be perfectly frank, doctor." St. John looked worn and anxious. "If there's any chance, I want you to take it."

"There might be a chance," Carter said thoughtfully. "I'm convinced, Mr. St. John, that you have no epilepsy, and I believe just as firmly that you owe all your trouble to the accident you speak of. The question is, are you strong enough to stand an operation?"

St. John smiled bitterly.

"That's not the only question," he said. "My idea of the situation is: which would be better, an operation now with a bare chance for recovery, or certain death in a few months?"

"I'm afraid that's about it?" Carter's voice was full of sympathy. "I can't offer a great deal of hope, but there's none the other way. The trouble is in the brain, of course—an old clot probably, and thickened membranes. But your stipulation is almost prohibitive. How in the world can we have an operation here without allowing your wife to know of it?"

I had had nothing to say before; now, however, I joined in the conversation.

"If you'll come up and do it. Carter, we can arrange the rest. I don't believe that it will do any good to deceive Mrs. St. John about it, but it won't do any harm either. She is wretchedly nervous anyhow, and it would be a strain for her."

"I'll come back, then," said Carter decisively. "Try and tone him up and strengthen him the next few days, Pierce, and I'll be up a week from tonight."

There was a certain solemnity in the farewell of the two men. Their next meeting meant life or death for one at the hands of the other. I was not sorry when we left the tense emotions of the sick room behind us and stood again under the stars.

"It's beastly luck," Carter said explosively, as we neared the trap. "I wouldn't say so in the house, but if Jamieson had showed a grain of intelligence he'd have operated two months ago, when that poor fellow was stronger."

The first part of the drive was quiet. Then Carter reached under the seat and pulled out a basket.

"Bully for the old gentleman," he said. "Here's claret and chicken, and by all that's holy, caviar sandwiches! Just thank him for me. Pierce, and tell him I'll send the catalogue he wants."

I drove slowly, and we discussed things while Carter ate the lunch. I told him of the mystery at Laurelcrest, and ended with the story of the changed capsules. When I finished we had passed the rectory and were almost at the hotel.

"It looks to me," he said lightly, as he prepared to descend, "as if the girl Georgia Ellis knows a good bit. She would seem to be the only person who could substitute one box for another."

"Except the nurse," I hazarded.

"Oh, the nurse—why, I've known Miss Martin for years, and she hasn't enough imagination to conceive such an idea. But I'm not a detective, old man—I'm a surgeon. Good-bye."

On my way home I puzzled over the problem with a heavy heart. Whatever meaning the presence of the empty pink box in the nurse's room might have, I had a faint recollection, every moment growing clearer, that the box Georgia Ellis gave me after our drive together was pink, not yellow.

During the long journey back to Laurelcrest I tried to arrange the events of the past few days. It was hard to remember that on Monday I had been busy with the usual routine of the hospital, and that in the short interval since—it was now Friday—the most important event of my life happened. I had fallen in love, not the sentimental folly of a boy in love with a pretty face, but the passion that comes only once—a love that shook me with its intensity and that drove me almost to frenzy when I remembered the look of guilt on Georgia Ellis's face the night St. John was poisoned.

<h1 style="text-align:center">CHAPTER TEN</h1>

"Look here, Mr. Hotchkiss," I said, the next morning after breakfast, "I'm a little uneasy about the responsibility I've taken in this house. We can't go ahead with that operation without consulting some of Mr. St. John's people. Suppose he doesn't pull through."

Hotchkiss stopped his nervous walk up and down the veranda, and frowned thoughtfully.

"His only relative, besides myself, is his father's sister, and she has lived in Dresden for a dozen years. As far as responsibility goes, Harry seems to have taken the thing into his own hands. There's no one to consult that I know except his wife, and she is barred."

"Miss Ellis," I suggested.

"Georgia's a nice girl, a very nice girl, Dr. Pierce. I like her as well as I like any woman, which isn't as much as it ought to be, perhaps. But if you don't want to tell Harry's wife, don't tell her best friend. It would slip out some way. As for the operation, it's Harry's privilege to make a decision that means more to him than to anyone else."

"I'll be glad when it's over," I said fervently. "With the best intentions in the world, the two sides of the family are deceiving each other; Mrs. St. John's brother and cousin arranged with her to conceal something from the other party, which seems to include, as you said the other day, an invalid, an—pardon me, I am quoting you—'an antediluvian fossil and a bit of a boy.' We seem bound to get the worst of it."

Hotchkiss chuckled. "Has Harry ever mentioned again the man who visited the car the night you lay over on the sidetrack?"

"Never," I said. "He has never referred to it, and he has never mentioned the fact that he saw Georgia Ellis the same night, when she took something from one of Miss Martin's bottles."

"For a good reason," he said assuredly. "For the best of reasons. He never mentioned that visit because it never occurred."

"You mean—?" I gasped.

"I mean," he replied enigmatically, "that Miss Martin is probably subject to nightmare."

I had not thought of such a possible solution before—not the solution the little man's words suggested, but the implication in his voice. Was it possible that Miss Martin had devised the story, with some object which I could not even surmise? And there was the incident of the box which I found in her bedroom.

"I'll venture to say," went on Hotchkiss, "that Harry has left her a tidy sum in his will."

"Not only that, but he intends to double it."

"Well," he said thoughtfully, "it's a very clever piece of work, and well carried out, but we'd better get rid of Miss Martin. If it was anyone but Harry, I would say let the thing go on until we could catch her red-handed. But I'm fond of Harry—he's a good boy—and we'd better dispense with the lady in the cap before she makes another error in his medicine."

"But the other things," I objected—"the light in the tower, the shriek, and the man who came to the car that night? Even granting that Miss Martin would commit a crime of that nature—which seems incredible—what do you make of these other things?"

Hotchkiss had been watching a flat stone near the edge of the veranda, where on sunny days an agile slate-colored salamander was accustomed to sun himself. Now with stealthy steps he stole down, his soft felt hat in his hand; but in the instant of the hat's descent, the little lizard had disappeared, and with a grunt of disappointment its would-be captor turned and came back.

"I would like to investigate the towers," he said, as if no interruption had occurred. "I heard Ellis and Miss Georgia arranging to go to Carson for some things, and Mrs. St. John is with her husband. By the way, I saw the clerk last night who filled your prescription, and he almost fell behind the counter when I told him I wanted to talk to him about the medicine he put up for the young lady from Laurelcrest. It seems Millard had been threatening him with the penitentiary. He declares that he filled your prescription exactly."

"So he did," I interrupted.

"And, moreover, that they haven't a pink box in the store. Therefore, whoever exchanged those boxes had brought the poison from the city, and only waited for an opportunity to administer the stuff."

"But if it should have been Miss—the person you suggested, why the capsules? Why not any of the drugs she had with her— the strychnia, or the chloral?"

I am afraid I fell in the estimation of Mr. Hotchkiss. He stopped poking with his pencil at a little bag of spider's eggs securely fastened in an angle of the wall, and turned to me sharply.

"You have the popular conception of crime," he sneered. "Why use a piece of wood from the woodpile when you have a revolver in your pocket? Why? Because any tramp could have used the wood, while the revolver at once incriminates you. The criminal worthy of the name avoids the obvious. Any member of the family could have made the exchange in the boxes—any drug-clerk be blamed for the error. Without such a possibility, the blame would have fallen on the nurse at once."

"But she raised the alarm."

"For one of two reasons—remorse, which is unlikely, or fear, which is probable."

It seemed plausible, and however unpleasant the task might be, I felt that it was necessary to send Miss Martin away at once. With our lack of proof against her it would be impossible to give anything like the true reason, and after her assiduous attention it was most difficult to trump up an excuse of any kind.

A groom drove up with the post-bag, and Hotchkiss sorted out the mail. "Four for Miss Georgia, mostly masculine writing," he said, "although these days when women use stub pens and spread all over the sheet, and men use fountain pens and write small for fear the ink gives out, it's confusing, sometimes. Here's a letter—two—for you, and one for somebody with a name between a cough and a sneeze. George, take this back to the housekeeper—it's probably for that Polish housemaid. And a telegram for me."

One of my letters was from Franklin, saying that there was a vacancy on the visiting staff, and I was being spoken of for the position. I don't mind saying I felt a trifle set up about it. There were a good many older men than I who would have given up almost everything but their hope of salvation for a position on the staff there. The other letter was from Jamieson. In small, cramped writing he acknowledged receipt of my letter, and begged to say that he saw no reason to change his opinion of Mr. St. John's case. Also, that he regretted that a bad attack of gout had convinced him that he would be better for a rest, and he would be at Wiesbaden about the tenth.

So my letter had gone—after all! And the unpleasant duty of telling Dr. Jamieson that his patient had decided to make a change in physicians was now no longer needful. It was one thankless task unnecessary.

"Fifty-three," said Hotchkiss thoughtfully. "I had no idea pink boxes were so popular with the drug trade."

"Fifty-three what?" I asked.

"Fifty-three drugstores in the city where they sell powders and capsules in pink boxes," he said disgustedly. "I hope there's a difference in shade, anyhow. You'll have to get that box for me, Pierce."

I agreed to make the attempt, and with the prospect before me of a stormy interview with Miss Martin, I went into the house.

At the foot of the big staircase I met Georgia Ellis. She was drawing off her gloves, and her face was flushed and troubled.

"Are you not going for your drive?" I asked, as she drew out the gold pins and took off her hat.

"I have decided not to go," she said. "I—I have a headache."

I thought she avoided my gaze, and it dawned on me, all at once, that she, like Mrs. St. John, was looking thin and worn. With a sudden impulse I held out my hand.

"Won't you let me help you?" I asked. "It's—it's more than I can stand to have you in trouble, and not be able to do anything."

She put her hand in mine, and it lay there for a moment. I wanted with all my heart to stoop and kiss the small fingers, but as if she divined my thoughts she drew it away quickly.

"I won't force a confidence," I said. "You have said it is not yours to give. But if I can do anything . . ."

"If I could trust anyone, I could trust you."

"Come out on the stone bridge," I suggested. "The air will help your headache, and I need an adviser."

She came willingly enough, as if it was a new and pleasurable thing to have someone to take the initiative. We went slowly under the trees, where the lawns were covered with fallen leaves and the borders, save where the chrysanthemums glowed near the shelter of the hedges, were bare and brown.

"I am always sad in the autumn," she said. "The trees are burying their children, and the poor old world looks so shabby and tired."

"It is time for Grandmother Nature to sit by the chimney," I said. "She has reared a large family this summer."

We walked on in silence to the bridge. Below, the little river clattered and splashed; the nasturtiums along the rail had been nipped by the frost, and hung their flaunting yellow heads. Georgia rested her arms on the cold stone, and drew a long breath.

"I am going away," she said slowly. "I'm going back home, Dr. Pierce, back to Kentucky." I was silent with sheer surprise.

"The worst of it is," she went on dully, "that I ought not to go; that I ought to stay here. But I cannot, I cannot!"

"Not soon?" I asked, my voice sounding strange and unnatural to my ears. She was going—going out of my life, when she had barely entered it! I would never see her again—never see that proudly uptilted chin, and the deep eyes with the black lashes. I squared my shoulders and looked across to where the greens of the mountains were beginning to show splotches of red and yellow.

"Very soon," she said sadly. "I am running away from something I ought to do, something I have given my word to do—and that is beyond my strength. I am deserting," she said, with a forced laugh. "Did you say you needed an adviser?"

"Yes, I need an adviser, I would like to have a friend, too," I hazarded. She made a little impatient gesture and I hurried on.

"I am going to make a change, Miss Ellis. Miss Martin will

leave this evening, and I want you to suggest a substitute, if either you or Mrs. St. John has a nurse you would care to employ. She should be a responsible woman—not a girl, and . . ."

"Miss Martin going?" Her astonishment was almost dismay.

"It is necessary," I said doggedly. "While I prefer to give her the benefit of the doubt, there were some peculiar circumstances connected with the error in medicines the other night. For one thing, the prescription was correctly filled at the pharmacy in Carson—the proper box turned up later, when the pink box with the poison capsules disappeared. Then, while looking for St. John's symptom chart in Miss Martin's room, I came across the pink box, empty."

She still leaned over the balustrade, her eyes fixed on the changing blues and whites of the sky reflected in the water below. But her fingers, which had been nervously tapping the edge of the flower-boxes, stopped suddenly, and her face was frozen and set.

"And one—might have—put the box in her room," she stammered, when the silence became oppressive.

"Not everyone would have a motive. Miss Martin is poor and middle-aged; she has thought, perhaps, that he would not live long."

"Do you think that?" she flashed at me.

"And she knows," I went on, ignoring the interruption, "that he has left her a certain amount of money in his will. You see we have even a motive."

"A motive that would apply to me also," she said bitterly. "I am a beneficiary, to a certain extent, in Harry's will. Why don't you suspect me?"

"I would as soon suspect my mother," I said fervently.

She stood up then and, turning around, looked straight in my eyes.

"Nevertheless," she said, and the world seemed to shatter and fall to pieces under my feet. "Nevertheless, Dr. Pierce, you must not send Miss Martin away. The error—it was an error—was mine! I gave you the pink box instead of the yellow one!"

She moved quickly across the bridge then, and I followed her. At the end she paused again. "Don't come with me," she said half-hysterically. "Don't ask me what I was doing with the other box—don't ask me anything. But for heaven's sake don't go away, doctor; whatever happens, don't leave these unfortunate people alone."

"But you are deserting," I said. "If I promise to stay, will you?"

"I cannot!" she shuddered.

"Tell me something," I pleaded. "Let me help you, as I wanted to before. The secret is safe with me. Wouldn't it be better to let me know it, whatever it is, than to have me going blindly along, stumbling over things I cannot understand, and not knowing whom to trust or distrust?"

"I cannot tell you," she repeated, "but if you will promise to stay, I will stay, too. I—I'm not a coward, whatever you think me."

"I think you everything that is good," I said gravely, "and I want you to know that whatever in the world you ask me to do I will do it, if the doing is possible."

"You are very good," she said, with a faint smile.

Then she left me, with my heart jumping like a triphammer, and the glow of her smile tingling all over me.

CHAPTER ELEVEN

The following day was Sunday. St. John had slept fairly well, and had been taken in a wheeled-chair to the glass-enclosed veranda which opened from his dressing room. From here he commanded a view of the drive, as it swept around toward the stables, and I found him amusing himself by watching the horses. The coachman, dressed in livery to drive the ladies to church, was supervising the showing off of the horses below their owner's window. Grooms and stable-boys were running around, leading stocky little cobs and slim, deep-chested hunters, while now and then a pair of shining carriage horses, stepping together, their heads proudly up, went sedately down the drive and back again. It was a sight to make a man's eyes sparkle, to watch that procession of beautiful horses, the younger ones frisking in the frosty morning air, the older ones moving with dignity, their muscles leaping into play under their polished skins.

St. John turned to me with shining eyes. "They've been my best friends," he said. "Next to my wife, almost my only friends."

We were both silent, watching the parade below. Finally the grooms led away the last horses, and the drive was deserted. St. John turned to me impulsively.

"You're keeping something from me, Pierce; I see a change in you. You're not sleeping, for one thing, and I'll venture you're not eating. What's the trouble?"

"There's nothing wrong with me," I said, trying to look unconcerned. "If I'm looking out of sorts, it's probably because I have been hunting imaginary troubles, and, not having your powers of imagination, I can't find them."

"You medical men make a specialty of covering a non-committal answer with a smother of words. Look here, Pierce, you were going to help me in this thing, and you are not doing it. You're trying to keep things from me, with a mistaken idea of shielding me, and instead, I am worrying more over the things I conjure up than I should over realities. Haven't you learned anything?"

I had foreseen this moment, when I gave my promise of secrecy about Ellis; I had feared it ever since, but now that it had come I was entirely unprepared.

"I am convinced there is a mystery," I said at last desperately, "but it seems to concern Georgia Ellis as much, or even more than your wife. I imagine that, when we have sifted the thing down, we will find less cause for anxiety than we think."

"You have learned nothing more about the man who visited the car that night?"

"Nothing," I answered truthfully enough, for while I might surmise that the man was Ellis, I had no absolute proof of the fact.

"There's something else, Pierce; if ever you run across a fellow prowling around the place here—a tall man, dark-eyed and sallow—I want you to let me know at once. It's unlikely, but it might happen, and in such a case I must know at once. If you can't come, send a message."

"A tall man, sallow and dark-eyed," I repeated mechanically.

"Yes—you won't find many strangers around here, and he's slightly stooped, so you will know him easily."

It was Ellis, beyond doubt. Dissimulation had always been hard for me, and now I found myself stammering like a schoolboy.

"But why—what—why should he prowl around here?" I asked. St. John twisted himself in his chair until he could face me squarely.

"I suppose," he said slowly, "that every family has some sort of skeleton hanging away; it happens that we have one. It is not a particularly grim affair, but it is a thing I am not at liberty to mention. I can tell you, however, that the man I have described is my wife's brother, and the fiancé of Georgia Ellis."

St. John's pale face seemed to grow blurred and indistinct against its pillows. Then I pulled myself together and managed to find an excuse for leaving the room.

The fiancé of Georgia Ellis! She loved him, then. She would marry him some day, and they would go away together, while—I stumbled to my room and threw myself into a chair. Well, it was all over; what use was ambition now, or hard work? I didn't want to succeed; I didn't want anything—but the girl I loved, and who belonged to another man. I sat there for an hour probably, in that condition between rage and black despair which is a man's substitute for tears. I heard the carriage start, taking the ladies to church, and watched Ellis go off for one of the long walks he took almost daily. I looked after him with a jealousy not unmixed with contempt. It was a blow to my self-esteem that I was defeated by so sorry a rival, for it seemed to me a feeble and almost shameful thing to hide, as he was doing, behind the petticoats of two women, living on the bounty of a man who despised him, and trading on the sympathies of the women who loved him. I gritted my teeth at the thought; I had even some wild idea of going down to his native state and hunting up the strange "politics," even in that country of political feuds, that could compel a man to hide in the mountains of Maine. But my hands were tied. St. John relied on me, and Friday would see either the beginning of a new lease of life for him or the end of everything.

In the midst of a reverie that was becoming painful Hotchkiss knocked at the door and came in. He was plainly excited, and he went directly to the window and watched Ellis as he tramped along a footpath which led toward the hills.

"Keeps out of sight of the west windows, doesn't he?" he chuckled.

I grunted some sort of a reply. Levity seemed out of place that morning, even levity as mild as that of Hotchkiss.

"It might be a good opportunity," he said, wheeling around suddenly, "to investigate the tower room this morning?"

I was willing, but not enthusiastic; the things I did know had faded into insignificance beside the one appalling fact that I did not know. However, anything was better than inaction, so I got up and drew a long breath.

"I suppose it's the best time," I said without enthusiasm. "Have you the keys?"

"I have some skeleton keys," he said. "We can get upstairs, always providing that there are no bolts."

"Bolts?" I asked curiously. "Why bolts, which would have to be pushed from the other side?"

Hotchkiss sat down then, and pulled out his little notebook, turning over the pages rapidly.

"Now," he said, "let's go over this thing coolly. In the first place, we will grant these girls a secret, which they are doing their best to hide. They didn't want to come here, for one thing. Why? Not because Ellis was here, for he is the brother of one and the cousin of the other. If he was hiding here, alone, they would be anxious to be with him. Well, in spite of all they can do, St. John insists on coming, and comes. The night the car lies over at the sidetrack Ellis comes down to consult with his sister. She has telegraphed him that they are coming, and it is necessary to take additional steps to guard this—this secret. Now—the family arrives and all goes well. It is easy to hide things from a sick man, and you and I and the nurse are told some cock-and-bull story which we swallow as a hen does a caterpillar. But there's a hitch some place. The secret, so well concealed, has a voice, and the evening of the day you arrive there's a shriek from the tower room overhead. There's been trouble of some sort; the three conspirators hurry to the tower room and pacify the secret. Georgia hears you downstairs, and being the bravest of the three—Ellis has no nerves—she undertakes to go down and throw you off the scent. In some way Mrs. St. John's arm has been cut and the blood is on Georgia's sleeve. She tells you a brave little lie about cutting her arm with a paper knife—and you believe it."

I had been growing more and more excited as he went on. Now, I seemed to see the whole situation in a glance.

"Then there's a fourth person!" I exclaimed. "Someone whom it is necessary to confine up there, and who may have escaped and . . ."

"Not too fast," he cautioned. "It's probable that there is a fourth to the trio who are, as you said before, banded together against St. John, you and myself. And I'm not prepared to say that this fourth person may not have been responsible for the attempted murder of St. John. But Georgia's attempt to take the responsibility would look like it."

"Then there's only one solution," I said eagerly. "The man, whoever it is, who is shut in the tower room is a maniac. Nothing else would explain that inhuman shriek and the murderous impulse. Great heavens! What a risk for the women to be running. Why, it must have been an attack of some sort that injured Mrs. St. John's arm."

"There's another thing that I have not yet mentioned," he went on, again consulting his notebook. "The night your friend Dr. Carter came up—last Friday, I believe—you will remember that I arranged to find him some sort of a luncheon."

"Yes. Go on," I said impatiently.

"Well, I went back as quietly as I could to Saunders's pantry, and as I pushed open the swinging-door I almost struck Mrs. St. John. The light was on, but she seemed to have had her hand on the switch button, and, as I opened the door, she turned it out. But she was not quite quick enough, for I had time to see a tray in her hand. She passed me with some little remark, and went upstairs. Now, you know that in itself is proof of a secret with an appetite. Had she herself wanted anything to eat she'd have sent that French maid of hers down to get it. It's the first time I have ever known of her going near the kitchen."

I began to have some scruples about investigating the upper rooms. What affair of ours was it to attempt the discovery of a secret that these people were guarding so carefully? Suppose we did discover a prisoner in the upper story, what then? Could I walk down and say to the women that I had discovered their precious secret—that I had obtained by force the confidence they refused to give me?

Hotchkiss, however, had no scruples.

"It is our affair," he said firmly. "It is a duty to save those girls from a possibility of harm, and besides, no matter of sentiment should keep a murderous lunatic from an asylum; St. John has had one experience: you or I may be the next. They are crafty, these insane."

Ellis had long disappeared from view, and time was passing.

With this new view of the case, that Georgia might be in danger, I was eager for the search. Hotchkiss got up and sorted over his skeleton keys.

"This," he said, "will open the staircase in this wing. It's not likely we will get much further, but we'll do what we can. Have you a revolver?"

I had, a 38-calibre Colt, and I stuck it in my pocket. Then we went quietly out and along the corridor. There was a Sunday calm all over the house. The white-capped housemaids, who were usually polishing the floors and flourishing dusters along the halls, had disappeared. No one saw us as we fitted the key into the white door of the staircase and turned it.

The door opened at once. Above us stretched the stairs, gleaming and bare, while a stained-glass window at the head threw red and blue and orange shadows on the white walls. It was rather cheerful than otherwise—there were no dark, shadowy corners with possibilities lurking in them; no cobwebs, no barred windows, no hollow groans. On the contrary, as we reached the top of the flight and turned to look around us, we found a scene very similar to the one we had left. There were the same long, broad corridors with shining floors and bright rugs; there was the same beautiful woodwork, the same vista of doors. The ceilings were lower, possibly—the rugs less costly, but the impression of cheeriness and sunlight was the same.

"I forgot to say," Hotchkiss said in a low tone, "that I learned from Harry that the rooms over yours are the hospital suite. The architect provided an isolation of rooms in case of contagious disease. It includes a bedroom, dressing room, bathroom and the tower alcove. There is a dumb-waiter, too, leading to the basement."

I nodded, and we went together toward the closed door

which led from the dressing room into the hall. It was locked, as was the door next, which led from the bathroom. Hotchkiss fumbled nervously with the keys, and his thin lips were quivering with suppressed excitement. He reminded me irresistibly of a fox-terrier who has chased a rat to his hole, and stands guard there, every muscle tense, and its stub of a tail quivering with excitement.

Finally I took the keys, and, after a few minutes' cautious manipulation, I succeeded in unlocking the dressing room door. I scarcely care to repeat my sensations as I opened it, inch by inch, and looked in. I expected a rush, a shriek, perhaps a blow—anything but the silence and emptiness that greeted us.

I pushed the door entirely open before we went into the room, and our progress was slow and extremely cautious. A minute sufficed to show the emptiness of the dressing room. Beyond its few pieces of furniture, a shaving stand, a chiffonier and a large wardrobe, it contained nothing but a chair or two. The bathroom was also empty. Here Hotchkiss pointed triumphantly to signs of recent occupancy; the soap in the nickel soap stand was soft and partly used, while a half-dozen towels lay round, incontrovertible evidence that the neat house maids of the rest of the house had no access here.

The door from the dressing room into the bedroom was not locked and here we exercised the greatest caution. If our theory held, the object of our search must be either in that room or in the tower alcove which opened from it. I am rather ashamed to confess that I was covered with cold perspiration when I put my hand on the knob of the door to open it. The pressure of the Colt in my pocket was comforting. I threw the door open and looked in. The bedroom, like the others, was empty.

Hotchkiss gave a comprehensive glance round—at the tumbled bed, at the stand nearby with a water bottle half full of water, and a glass, then he pointed to the corner. There, as in the rooms below, portieres hung over the entrance to the tower alcove. Convinced that the mystery, secret, whatever it might be called, lay beyond the curtains, I summoned my courage—it's a question of moral, not physical courage when you are about to face the unknown—and drew the curtains aside.

We faced, not the circular alcove with small, high windows that we had expected to find, but instead a heavy door, closed and locked.

Hotchkiss stooped down and examined the fastening. It was a square bronze plate, very heavy and without a keyhole, while a very small knob, perhaps an inch and a half across, proved its nature. Hotchkiss turned it once and listened to the click. With all my experience in such matters, I knew it to be a combination lock. The room in the tower was as safe from intrusion as a banking vault, and the mystery was as far from solution as ever.

There was no sound from beyond the heavy door, and we tiptoed out and locked the door behind us. Then we went softly down the stairs again and into my apartments below.

For an hour we discussed the various aspects of the case. Whatever doubt there might have been before, there seemed room for none now. There was a prisoner in the tower room, a prisoner who was restrained by force; more than that we knew nothing. And as we talked we realized that there were some things still unexplained. How had the prisoner succeeded in obtaining the poison, and how succeeded in exchanging the pink for the yellow box?

CHAPTER TWELVE

Ellis came back late in the afternoon. I chanced to meet him on the stairs, and was shocked by the change in his appearance. I had little reason to like him, but his ghastly face aroused my professional interest.

"What's wrong, Ellis?" I asked as he tried to brush past me. "Are you ill, or have you ad bad news?"

"It's a combination of both," he said, avoiding my eyes, "only I'm not ill; I'm simply worn out."

I let him pass me then, and went on down the stairs, but was certain I heard him go to the locked staircase, and later I had proof of it. He did not appear at dinner, and when I mentioned his altered appearance I intercepted a quick exchange of glances between Georgia Ellis and her cousin—glances full of consternation and dismay. If Hotchkiss noticed anything, he did not say. He went on at length with the life history of a small, green snake that he had once hatched in a chicken incubator, and which he declared had learned to beg for food, and dinner passed off rather well.

Hotchkiss and I took our afternoon smoke in the billiard room, he, in his characteristic fashion, pacing up and down with his hands behind him, while I aimlessly knocked the balls about and chewed at the end of my unlighted cigar. After a while I stopped, and going over to the fireplace, broached the subject that was never out of my mind.

"I have just learned," I said, with what I considered a fine assumption of indifference, "that Miss Georgia is engaged to Ellis. Did you know it?"

"Bless my soul, no!" he said. "Why, I—you will excuse an old man, Pierce, and it's none of my business, but I had an idea that you and Georgia had fixed things up between you."

"Well, you were wrong," I said gruffly. Then, half-ashamed of my humor, I went on more civilly: "For one thing, I'm not an eligible in any sense; I've nothing but my profession, no money."

"Neither has he," interrupted Hotchkiss, "and no profession, either. Lives on his sister's bounty. I'll be blessed if I can understand women."

"He's a handsome devil, too," I went on, touching on that delicate topic of appearance which we all profess to scorn. Hotchkiss started to interrupt me again, but I hurried on. "Anyhow, it isn't a question of either money or looks; the girl loves him. You can't deny it," I challenged him. "Look how often they are together; to see one is to see the other. They drive, walk, read . . ."

"Nonsense," said Hotchkiss. "They have the tie of a common interest, a common secret—that's all. I tell you if I was a young fellow and in love, I wouldn't want to see contempt in the girl's eyes, and there's contempt there, most of the time."

The door into the hall opened to admit Saunders and closed behind him. He was looking at Hotchkiss and I noticed that his face was as white as his spotless shirt front.

"We've heard them again, sir," he said, half-leaning against the door. "They're worse than usual, and the boy that minds the furnaces has fainted away, sir."

Hotchkiss threw away the end of his stogie—he smoked

Pittsburg stogies, and the very smell made my hair rise—and started for the door.

"Come on, Pierce," he called over his shoulder. "We are going settle the Laurelcrest ghost."

He was manifestly excited. There was a new erectness in his narrow shoulders, a triumphant inflection to his voice, and with the prospect of action my spirits lightened. Saunders led the way to the back of the house, and we followed close on his heels. Through the breakfast room, past the servants' dining room, and back to the big tiled kitchen, where a dozen of the house servants were gathered in a subdued, whispering crowd. Every light was turned on—the room was as bright as daylight, and a copper kettle hummed cheerfully on the big range which filled one side of the room. But the atmosphere was tense with horror, and there was fear, the awful, wide-eyed fear of the unknown, on every face.

On the floor in the center of the room lay the grimy figure of the furnace boy, a lad of about nineteen, now partly conscious, but refusing to get up, and lying crouched there in abject terror. I bent over him and felt his pulse, which was galloping furiously.

"He's been that way since he came up," said the cook, a slim little woman. "He just fell through that door there and rolled over on the floor. Once before he came up that way, yelling that there were ghosts in the cellar, and I ain't been down there since."

The crowd huddled closer together, and one of the house-maids began to whimper.

Hotchkiss went to the door the cook indicated, and slipped back the bolt. Quick as thought Saunders was before him, his hand on the knob.

"For God's sake, don't go down, Mr. Hotchkiss!" he said shakenly. "There's something wrong, sir. The house is haunted; the doctor can tell you about the shriek we heard one night, and there's something moaning now, in the cellar, under the east wing."

"I hope there is," said Hotchkiss cheerfully. "Come on, Pierce. Is it lighted down there, Saunders?"

Saunders muttered something which we construed as yes, and throwing open the door, Hotchkiss was about to lead the way down.

I stepped ahead of him, however, with the feeling that however ghostly the sounds might be, there was a chance that physical strength would be needed, and that my bulk was better fitted to meet a sudden onslaught than Hotchkiss's slender frame. Hotchkiss turned at the door to the open-eyed crowd behind us.

"Not a word of this," he said threateningly. "Get about your business, all of you. Turn out some of these lights and go back to your rooms—play cards, anything—say your prayers if you want to, but not a word of this upstairs. Saunders, will you come down, or will you wait here? "

Saunders hesitated between Hotchkiss's scornful smile and the shadows of the basement stairs. Then he gulped once or twice.

"I think I'll not go, Mr. Hotchkiss," he said weakly, "my nerves are bad, and I'd be no use, sir."

We started down alone, then, and smiled as we reached the foot of the stairs to hear the door softly closed behind us. Cut off suddenly from even the feeble support of the kitchen, the situation was decidedly eerie. The cellars dimly lighted, white-walled, stretched around us in a decreasing perspective of lights and black shadows; our steps echoed hollowly on the cement flooring, and. from some place in the distance came the muffled whir of the machinery in the engine room. We went there first, skirting around the dynamos which lighted the house, peering back of the big engine which chilled the refrigerating-room, and then, beyond, to where the big force pump, gleaming with brass and dripping with oil, sent water up through the house. There was no one around. The old Scotchman who tended the engines was upstairs with the rest of the terrified household, and we went on alone, through the laundry and the big drying rooms; through the big empty space reserved for the unbuilt swimming pool, and into the unused places beyond, where our footsteps sounded hollow in the emptiness and where only an occasional light here and there accentuated the shadows. We were in the room under the east wing, and were about to give up and go back, when we heard a sound. It was inarticulate at first, growing louder gradually, until it sounded like a muffled human voice, and ending with a wail that faded slowly, slowly into a quivering silence, and left our nerves throbbing with its acute anguish.

"Great heavens!" I gasped. "Where was that?"

Hotchkiss pulled himself together with an effort, and stared around him. The sound had been followed by a silence which to our strained ears was pregnant with possibilities. The rhythmic beat of the engines sounded faintly in the distance, but around us was gloom and quiet, and I could hear the blood rushing through my ear drums.

"There's somebody hiding around here," said Hotchkiss, his voice sounding sepulchral in the silence. "Where there's a voice there's a throat to produce it, that's certain." He began to move cautiously around the walls and I followed him. Together we examined every corner without result. Then Hotchkiss stopped and looked round.

"This must be under the hall," he said thoughtfully, "and the dark corner there is beneath the tower. By Jove," excitedly, "I know the whole thing now. Have you matches?"

I had half a dozen or so, and with the aid of one, carefully shielded with his hand, we groped our way into the gloomy recess he had pointed out. It was as he had surmised; the semi-circular wall showed that it lay beneath the tower, and with his unoccupied hand Hotchkiss pointed to a small doorway in the stone.

"The dumb-waiter to the hospital suite," he whispered. "Listen."

The match flickered and went out, and as I fumbled for another a laugh issued from the partly open door. A horrible maniacal laugh that seemed to come from the obscurity around us, and that froze the blood in my veins. Then silence again.

I think I should have run had not Hotchkiss found an electric lamp near and turned the switch. In the light that followed we were ready to face anything, and we waited expectantly, close by the door of the shaft, for a repetition of the sounds. But none came. After perhaps thirty minutes of tension I sat down on the cold floor and tried to make myself comfortable while Hotchkiss took out his notebook and made methodical entries.

An hour went by, two hours, and not a sound from the tower room had come down the shaft. Hotchkiss had brought a chair from the engine room and dozed comfortably, waking up now and then when his head dropped with a jerk, then dropping off again. I got stiff after a time, and tried walking up and down for a change, always, however, with an eye and an ear for the little door in the wall.

I thought over a good many things in that long vigil; of the difference between myself as I had left the hospital a few days before, and the Carroll Pierce of the present, wildly in love with a girl who loved another man, conspiring against her for the discovery of a secret she was helping to guard, busying myself, in other words, with other people's affairs; not even entirely frank with St. John, who trusted me; and assisting in his deception of his wife as I assisted her in deceiving him. Truly it was not an enviable position, and with St. John's operation approaching and the discovery, which seemed imminent, of a murderous maniac in the tower room, I began to feel that the position was scarcely bearable.

It was about midnight when Hotchkiss roused himself and got up yawning.

"Our friend has gone to sleep," he said, nodding toward the closed door. "I'm going upstairs to see if there's a light in the tower windows, and to get a book. Then you can doze and I'll take my turn at watching."

I sank into his chair and watched his disappearing frame as he went toward the stairs, then, with my legs stretched out and my hands in my pockets, I went on with my usual reflections.

Suppose the operation was a success and St. John began to go around again? What would become of Ellis? What would they all do with the prisoner in the tower room? What would I do if this unknown should attack and injure Georgia Ellis?

A slight sound attracted my attention. It was a scraping like the heel of a boot on a board, and at first I could not locate it. Then, all at once, I knew. It came from the shaft of the dumb-waiter, and even as the conviction forced itself on me I saw the handle of the door turn and open about an inch.

I raised in my chair and leaned forward, ready to spring. My heart seemed to have stopped and every nerve centered in one ominous object—that slowly opening door. And then the lights went out. Not gradually, but suddenly, leaving me in utter blackness, my eyes straining, my tongue dry, my hands clutched and tingling. There was perfect silence—then a sudden shriek close by me. I think I shrieked, too. Then there was a rush, a wave of air as a body ran past me, a far-off moaning call, and silence.

And I sat in that black darkness, unable to find my way out, with that awful shriek ringing in my ears, with flashes of light streaking the darkness to my overstrained eyes, while I shivered with the cold terror of the unknown.

CHAPTER THIRTEEN

The lights flashed up again in an instant, but there was no one to be seen. I hurried through the different rooms, only to be met with emptiness. Once, indeed, I thought I heard muffled footsteps, and I ran in the direction from which they seemed to come, only to meet with disappointment. When, at last, I found a flight of steps that led outside, with the door at the top open, I knew that search was useless; the creature, man, woman or beast, had made its escape. Still shaken with my experience, I went slowly upstairs to find Hotchkiss.

We met in the back hallway, and I could see that he was as much excited as I.

"Something has happened," he said hurriedly. "I don't know whether to offer assistance or not—they are so peculiar about this thing. But I imagine the prisoner has escaped; I met Ellis running over the lawn, only half dressed, and Georgia Ellis just now came down the front staircase, as white as death."

"I'm going to her," I said, pulling away from his grasp on my arm. "He—or she—has escaped. Somebody slid down the cable of the dumbwaiter just as the lights went out, and flew past me. Don't try to keep me; there may be murder done while we stand here."

I hurried to the front of the house. The lights were low and everything was quiet, but at the far end of the veranda I saw a slender, white-clad figure and I went toward it. In the faint starlight there was no more—I saw Georgia Ellis, crouching against the stone balustrade, her eyes peering into the black shadows of the trees on the lawn, one hand clutching nervously at her throat. She did not move when I touched the hand on the balustrade, and I saw she was shivering violently.

She was dressed as she had been that evening, in something soft and white, and its loose half-sleeves and low-cut neck were no protection from the cold night air.

"You must come in, Georgia," I said imperatively. "Standing here will do no good, and you are simply courting pneumonia. Come in, little girl."

She did not look at me. She shook her head impatiently, and gazed across the lawn. I stood beside her for a minute, uncertain what to do. Unwelcome as I was, it was out of the question to leave her there alone, exposed to heaven knows what danger, chilled with cold, troubled and anxious as she was. After a bit I went into the house and brought down my raincoat, which I wrapped around her shoulders. Then I drew up a chair, and she sank into it with a little sigh of fatigue.

We sat there for half an hour, I on the balustrade, my eyes on the faint outline of her face, holding myself back with an effort. If only it had been my privilege, my right, to have knelt beside her there, slipping my arm around her, to have comforted her, sending her off to bed and taking her place as I longed to do. But she belonged to another man; it was for his safe return from 'this unknown danger that she prayed and waited. Down under the trees somewhere he was following up the fugitive and like the onlookers in a play, we were forced to sit and watch—and wait.

The raincoat slipped down from her white shoulders and I drew it around her tenderly. She roused a little, then, and I saw with relief that the strained look was leaving her eyes.

"It's such a comfort to have you here," she said simply. "I'm afraid I'm a coward."

"It is more than that to me to be here," I said. "It is harder than you know to see you in trouble and to realize that I can never be anything but an outsider."

"An outsider?" she questioned.

"I could not expect to be anything else. I want too much. I should not even be satisfied with friendship, and I am not your friend."

"I had hoped you were," she said wistfully.

"Friendship implies confidence; you deny me even the small comfort of helping you bear your troubles," I said brutally. "I don't mean I would be satisfied with the crumbs from the table, but I would take them; a famishing dog will take anything."

"I think I need a friend." She leaned back in her chair and closed her eyes. "Wherever I look I see only endless complications, endless mystery, endless secrecy. There is sickness and the dread of death in the west wing, and in the east wing."

"What?" I bent toward her eagerly.

"Trouble—trouble that I cannot tell you," she said wearily. "I am going in now. It will soon be morning, and there is no use in staying longer." She got up and slipped off my raincoat and gave it to me. "I cannot tell," she said, "but perhaps by tonight you will know our trouble, and I will be glad—glad."

She gave me her hand, and I took it fervently in both of mine. "I believe that things are going to come right for you," I said as cheerfully as I could. "They will never come right for me."

I did not go to bed that night. For a time I walked round the trees, stopping at the stone bridge to look back at the house. In the tower room over mine there was a bright light, but no figure appeared at the windows, and everything was quiet. Once I was startled to hear stealthy footsteps near and I stood close to the trunk of a big beech, in the shadow, until Hotchkiss emerged into an open space near and looked round. He was manifestly startled when I spoke to him, but concealed it well, and we went back to the house together.

"There's no use in staying up," he said. "The prisoner has got away, probably for good. Ellis is hunting through the neighborhood, but he might as well be in his bed. The whole thing is bound to come out tomorrow, and if we are to be of any account we'll be the better for a few hours' rest."

It seemed probable he was right; the secrecy, so carefully maintained by Ellis and the two women, could no longer be maintained if a dangerous maniac were at large in the vicinity.

Outside help would have to be called in, the thing would be in the papers and we would be fortunate indeed if we should succeed in keeping it from St. John.

Before I went to my room I slipped into the sick man's bedroom. Everything was quiet and dark, but St. John himself was wakeful and alert. He raised himself on his pillows as I came in, and motioned me to close the door into the next room, where Miss Martin, in a slate-gray negligee, lay sleeping heavily on a couch.

"It's three o'clock," he said when I had done so, "and you are dressed, Pierce. What's wrong?"

It was too late to repeat my indiscretion, and I made the best excuse I could.

"I wasn't sleeping," I said, "so I have been walking around. Have you been awake long?"

"I haven't slept at all," he said, with a shade of resentment in his tone. "Why these evasions. Pierce? Am I never to have the truth? There is something wrong in the house tonight, and instead of coming here and telling me what has occurred, you walk in at three o'clock in the morning, in a dinner coat and black tie, and expect me to believe that when you don't sleep you always rig yourself out that way to walk around. I wish you would treat me as a rational human being."

I drew a chair beside the bed and sat down.

"I haven't been as frank as I ought to be," I said. "The fact is that the servants in the house think the cellar is haunted, and Mr. Hotchkiss and I have been down there for hours. There are mysterious noises—we heard them—capable, of course, of a solution. We've been hunting the solution, that's all."

"That's about half," he said grimly. "I suppose that's what my wife was doing about midnight when she rushed in here, as white as paper, and rushed out again, without a word to me. You see, I know more than you expected."

"1 didn't know that myself," I assured him, "and while I suspect some things, Mr. St. John, I know as little now as when I came to Laurelcrest. I believe that there is a mystery, but I also believe it will be cleared up in a day or two, and it will be better to wait for it to solve itself than for me to force your wife's confidence and incur her dislike."

"I suppose so," he said wearily, "but I would like to clear things up before the operation, and another thing, this strain, whatever it is, is telling on Mrs. St. John's mind; she is acutely melancholy. If—if anything happens to me, Pierce, I want you to look after her. Stay with her until the first shock is over, and help her out of this other trouble, too."

"I will," I said. "I don't expect anything to happen, but if it does, I give you my promise to stand by her and help her, as I would want someone to care for my wife if I had one."

"You're a good fellow, Pierce." He held out his hand and I

took it. "I have felt from the first moment that I could trust you, and I do now. I have gone through so much in the past months that the end would be a relief, if it were not for leaving her. Some day you will know what it is to love one woman more than all the world, and I hope you will never have to lie helpless and see her in the very extremity of mental suffering and be unable to help her."

As I went back to my room his words echoed through my mind—for even now I loved one woman more than all the world, and although she was suffering, I was as unable to help her as though I lay tied on St. John's bed.

CHAPTER FOURTEEN

I was somewhat disturbed the next morning, or rather the same morning—I went to bed at four and was up at nine—to find my revolver missing from the top of my shaving stand. At first I thought one of the housemaids had mislaid it, although it seemed rather improbable, for so great was their fear of it that the top of the shaving stand had gone undusted since I had placed it there. I looked for it in every spot, likely or unlikely, where a courageous housemaid might have hidden it, but without result. The revolver was gone.

I breakfasted alone. Saunders said the ladies had breakfasted in their rooms and Hotchkiss had had coffee at seven and had driven over to Carson. I do not think he went to bed at all that night. Both sleeping and eating became minor considerations when his zeal was aroused, and I imagined that the trip to Carson was an excuse, and that he was really scouring the country for some trace of the fugitive.

Sometime about noon Mr. Wheatly, the lawyer, came out from town, and he spent most of the afternoon with St. John. I passed a restless day, seeing no one, unable to read or bowl, and waiting for developments that did not materialize. No frightened country people had come in with tales of ghostly visitor the night before; there had been no crime committed; no eerie figure had been seen flitting in the gray light between night and morning. Of course, it was probable that the fugitive was lurking somewhere in the mountains, and that another day or so would see his discovery. In the meantime 1 walked the verandas restlessly, waiting and watching for I knew not what.

Sometime in the afternoon I went down to the cellars again and went over the ground inch by inch. The old Scotchman, half ashamed, was at his post in the engine room, and from him I got a candle, a hammer and some nails. Then I went back to the dark recess where 1 had kept vigil the night before and where the overturned chair still bore mute evidence to the haste with which I left it.

Here I struck a match and lighted the candle, preparatory to fastening up the door of the shaft. Improbable as it seemed, it was possible that Ellis would find the fugitive, and under cover of darkness bring him back to his prison. In such an event his escape must be prevented until Hotchkiss and I could decide on some plan of action.

I opened the door and, holding the candle inside the shaft, examined it carefully. The slide itself, a heavy affair, box-shaped and containing two shelves, was dropped below the level of the doorway and seemed to rest on the bottom of the shaft, thus leaving the doorway free. A thick wire cable was fastened securely to the top of the box, and ascended entirely to the roof. It was easy then to explain the descent of the fugitive, a descent sufficiently perilous to daunt a sane mind, for the slide, which might have served as an elevator, had been fastened down with heavy nails driven into the wood of the shaft. Something white was lying on top of the box now, and I held the candle close to it. It was a woman's handkerchief, with a faint scent of violet still clinging to it. I slipped it into my pocket for closer inspection later. Then I put the candle on the floor and prepared to nail up the door. I took another look up the dark shaft, and without the rays of the candle to confuse me, I was able to see what I had not noticed before—far up in the blackness was a narrow point of light, and quite suddenly I realized that the way lay open to the locked room in the tower. Even if the bird had flown, there might be some bits of plumage in the empty cage.

It was not difficult to remove the nails. I noticed what might have indicated many things to Hotchkiss, but meant nothing to me. The nails were bent and awkwardly driven, with marks around where the hammer had missed its aim. Later, I understood the pathos of those hastily driven nails. Freed of the restraint, the cage moved easily and without noise, by means of a second cable running along the walls. It was quite possible, therefore—providing the builders had done their work well—to stand on the top of the box and ascend safely to the upper floor.

I resolved to make the attempt. There seemed to be no danger with the prisoner missing, but once past the doorway and the light of the candle, moving slowly upward in the three-foot shaft with all the possibilities that lurked behind the spot of daylight above, I began to wish that I had my lost revolver in my pocket.

About halfway up a new thought struck me: suppose Ellis had found the prisoner and had smuggled him into the house while I slept? I would be trapped like a rat, my escape cut off, while a murderous creature from above could drop heavy furniture on me, shoot me, scald me—I pulled myself together and gave the cable a determined pull. Occupied or empty, I was going to see the interior of the tower room.

As I got close to the opening I went more slowly, bringing the cage to a standstill, while only my head and shoulders were above the floor. The door was partly open, and I could see perhaps half of the room. It was apparently empty; the floor was littered with bits of cotton and a chair lay overturned near me. Directly across was the door which had barred out Hotchkiss and myself the day before, but it was not that which gripped my attention and kept me wide-eyed with amazement. On the floor at the door sill lay a handcuff unlocked and separated from its mate, and beside it, just at the limit of my field of vision, the narrow toe of a woman's slipper.

Even as I looked the foot moved a little and I could see now the arched instep, the buckle, the frivolous little heel, that belonged to slippers I had seen Georgia Ellis wearing. I scarcely dared to move. She was sleeping, of that I felt certain, for in the absolute quiet of the house I could hear her regular breathing. With infinite caution I pushed the door a little wider open and looked at the strange scene before me.

Georgia Ellis was sitting on a low couch, leaning back, her shoulders against the wall, her head drooping a little to one side, soundly sleeping. She was still in the white gown she had worn all the night before, and her hair was loosened and disheveled. Even in sleep her small mouth had a pathetic droop, and her face was as colorless as her gown. The room itself was in the most amazing condition; bits of the wall-paper had been stripped away, showing the plaster beneath; a plate and cup lay in fragments on the floor, and there were scraps of cotton and lint scattered over the heavy Persian rug. And in the midst of the ruin Georgia Ellis slept quietly on, the lace of her gown moving with every breath, a cold wind from the open window blowing over her bare arms.

I think it was the wind that aroused me to the necessity of action. It was inviting death to allow her to sit there in that costume, and although it involved a risk of discovery, I determined to close the window and throw over her the little shawl that lay on the ground at her feet. I raised the slide a few feet, and prepared to carry out my plan. With my hand on the door to the shaft, however, I paused. Someone was working with the combination lock of the door into the room; the handle turned once or twice, with a resulting click, and Georgia moved uneasily. I hesitated for a moment, uncertain whether to stay and thus force the issue, or to retreat. I believe the dislike I felt to my unwelcome role as spy was responsible for the decision. To have Georgia discover me in my present position was something I had not counted on. And as she moved wearily in response to the clicking lock I closed the door of the shaft and pulled the cable for the descent.

The trip had been one of little avail; true, the condition of the room had shown that our theory of a dangerous maniac was more than a theory—witness the handcuff. But it told me that the recapture of the fugitive was confidently expected, and that Mrs. St John and Georgia would probably be again subjected to the perils incident to caring for him.

I fastened the door at the foot of the shaft, and returning the tools to the engine room, went upstairs to my room. My coat was dusty from the walls of the shaft, and I needed a bath and a change of linen after my trip. I found Hotchkiss in my little tower den, leaning back in a reclining chair and pondering over the big anatomy book as if he had no other interest in the world. On the floor he had arranged a couple of pillows from my bed, ends toward the window, in the rough semblance of a man, and I saw with amusement that he had drawn on one the rough outline of a human thorax, ribs, lungs and heart. "I've been thinking about the Carrol case," he said, blinking at me over his glasses. "The bullet was flattened, you remember, and the medical expert said it had hit a rib. Now this was the cause," he went on, bending over the pillow and indicating with his pencil, "the man was sleeping on the floor, the course of the bullet was at an angle of forty-five degrees from the surface and they are going to hang a man who was riding past, fifty yards away at the time. If he had been in a balloon we might account for it, but on horseback—bosh! I am convinced that the bullet was fired from just below the window, struck the frame which flattened it and ricocheted into Carrol's heart. And the man who did it has been the star witness at the trial."

"It's very interesting," I said, fumbling in my pockets and producing the handkerchief, "but I wish you would use some of your inductive reasoning on this. I found it at the foot of the shaft in the cellar."

Hotchkiss turned it over curiously, taking it to the window for closer inspection. Then he put it in his pocket.

"Have you ever thought, Pierce," he said, "that this prisoner might have been a woman?

There are some things that make me think it. For one thing, the face you saw at the tower window the night you arrived was a woman's. Why need we suppose it to have been either Harry's wife or Georgia Ellis? And your description of the shriek that night sounded like the high, piercing scream of a woman. Now the handkerchief certainly looks that way. Besides, if it were a woman, it would be easier to understand the part these two girls have been playing."

It was a new possibility to me, but it really meant little. Whether man or woman, the condition of the tower room had revealed enough to make me hope that the escape had been final —that Ellis would not succeed in finding and bringing back the maniac. I shuddered at the terrible scenes Georgia Ellis must have witnessed, and when I had told Hotchkiss of my trip on the dumbwaiter, and what I had seen, he was visibly disturbed.

"It is absurd to see such a state of affairs in a sane house- hold," he said, slamming shut the anatomy book and putting it away. "The only thing I can think of is to keep a close watch on the house, and to prevent Ellis bringing anyone in. But we can arrange later about tonight; in the meantime you would better dress and look around for Wheatly. He was asking for you." It was after five then and I did not see Mr. Wheatly until dinner. He was a tall, slender man, iron-gray, with shrewd eyes and a kindly smile. I rather took to him, and we talked over the question of malpractice suits, both the medical and the legal standpoint. Mrs. St. John did not appear at dinner, and Georgia was very quiet at the table. Hotchkiss joined in only occasionally. Ellis's place was empty.

After dinner Wheatly and I continued our discussion over very excellent cigars of his own providing. I have found that most lawyers have good tobacco and good clothes. Whether they are the result of success or its cause, is a question. But Wheatly's cigars were unimpeachable, and under his practical, matter-of-fact conversation some of the uneasiness melted away. But he had something to say to me, and after a few minutes he approached the matter.

"About this operation," he said abruptly. "St. John is determined on it, and, of course, no one can deny him his chance for life. But there is one thing I don't approve of, Dr. Pierce, and that is, his running such a risk without telling his wife, or at least some of her people."

"I think as you do about it, Mr. Wheatly," I said, lowering my voice, for the library windows were just beside us, "but he is firm. And, as you say, it is his one chance for life. Then, of course, in one way he is justified. Mrs. St. John is nervous and excitable. It would be a fearful ordeal for her."

"She looks very badly," he said, turning around to get a good view of my face. "Is it physical—or mental? "

"Both," I said evasively. "I do not believe she has ever been strong, and lately there has seemed to be something on her mind."

He nodded. "Better not tell her, then; if I remember correctly, there is insanity in her family.

But it will be better to consult some members of either side of the house, I imagine. If anything goes wrong, with the amount of the estate involved, and the other issues, it will be better to have the support of the family."

"I have already spoken to Mr. Hotchkiss, Mr. St. John's uncle."

"Very well. Then I advise you to consult with some member of his wife's family. It is, as I say, for your own protection."

I thought over his advice later in the evening, when, by prearrangement with Hotchkiss, I strolled the lawns and shrubberies. Unpleasant as was the thought of consulting Ellis on any subject pertaining to St. John, it seemed the only thing to do. Whatever opinion I might have of him as a successful rival and a parasite on the bounty of a man who despised him, the fact remained that he was still Mrs. St. John's brother and closest relative. And Wheatly's advice was sound. It was Monday night; in four days Carter would arrive, ready for his part of the work, and whatever I had to do must be done quickly.

Still debating the matter, I went over to the stone bridge, and leaning on the parapet, smoked meditatively. I had not been there since the day Georgia Ellis and I had stood there together, and the memory came back vividly. I thought I understood now what she meant when she said that she was going away, that she ought not to go, but she must; that she was deserting—running away from something that was beyond her strength. I began to understand, too, some of the mystery of the pink box. It had contained an opiate, probably for the insane creature in the tower room, and she had made an error in the boxes. What I did not understand, and what I began to fear I should never understand, was the reason for all the secrecy. Why should three people, all otherwise apparently reasonable, conspire to keep such a person out of an asylum for the insane? And why—why—did Mrs. St. John not confide in the husband who loved her so well?

CHAPTER FIFTEEN

About midnight, as nearly as I could tell—I did not wish to attract attention by striking a match to look—I saw Ellis. He came on foot, as he had gone, and although there was only faint starlight, I fancied that he walked as though he were exhausted. I could imagine the condition he was in after his hopeless search, but he would probably have resented even a covert offer of sympathy, so I drew back into the shadow and watched him. He did not go in at once, but stood looking around, and for a moment I thought he had seen me. But he turned after a while and went slowly into the house, and by moving along the east wing I saw the lights flash up in his room.

Breakfast the next morning was more cheerful. Ellis looked tired, but was in better spirits than I had expected. Georgia, too, looked brighter, although I watched in vain for the little intimate glances that might be expected between lovers. Mrs. St. John did not appear; she had kept her room since the night of the prisoner's escape, but as I had not been called in professionally I was forced to conclude that her trouble was of the mind, not of the body.

Hotchkiss had had an early breakfast, as he had done the day before and had gone for a long cross-country walk. He was a little man, without the slightest muscular development, but he could do more on pure nervous energy than I could with a hundred and eighty pounds of gymnasium-trained muscle.

After breakfast I made my morning visit to the sick room. Just now, in spite of what the future held in store, it was the most cheerful place in the house. Miss Martin was sitting near a window with some gray yarn in her lap, and without knowing just where the change lay, I recognized an alteration in her appearance—perhaps it was her hair, I'm sure I don't know— that was infinitely coquettish; she looked less a machine and more a woman, and I recollected suddenly that two or three times in the last few days I had seen her taking her daily stroll along the drive, with Mr. Hotchkiss beside her, his nervous walk accelerating her more leisurely footsteps until she would come in panting, with heightened color and shining eyes.

I chatted for a few minutes with St. John and then walked over and picked up the wool lying in Miss Martin's lap. "They look a little small for me," I said. "I presume, of course, they are intended as my Christmas gift."

She laughed consciously. "They are not a Christmas gift for anyone; I—I rather thought of giving them to Mr. Hotchkiss. He complains of cold feet at night."

St. John smiled at me over his book. I am afraid I was amused myself; for some unaccountable reason, the romance of the middle-aged always excites the ridicule of the young and the scorn of the old. I am more tolerant now; I find that, like beauty, age is only as deep as its wrinkles and gray hairs, and that the heart is often young when the stomach is in its dotage and the liver is fossilized with years. But to this minute I cannot think of the affair between Miss Martin and Mr. Hotchkiss without a smile.

I stood with the knitted bed shoe in my hand, looking at the bit of woodland beyond the window. It was a dull, gray day, windy and cold, and the heap of nuts on the windowsill was untouched. Under the trees outside the fallen leaves swirled and eddied in each fresh gust of wind and there was a feeling of snow in the air. It was then that I saw the man in the gray suit. For a moment I was uncertain, for he was at a considerable distance from the house, and the gray of his clothing faded indeterminately into the colorous background of leaves and tree trunks.

Then he moved, and I saw him distinctly. I could make out from his gestures that he was smoking, and imagine, rather than see, the flash of the match.

Miss Martin was again busy with her work, and no one had seen the stranger. I felt a chill of apprehension, although my better judgment told me that this equable, pipe-smoking visitor could not be the escaped maniac from the tower room. Even granting that, however, there was something ominous in the man's furtive scrutiny of the house, and as soon as I could get away I took my hat and went out.

With Miss Martin at the window, it was out of the question to go directly to the spot where I had seen the man. Instead I went out a back door, made a detour round the stables and came, in ten minutes or so, within sight of the place. But quick as I had been, the man had been quicker. The leaves were trampled where he had been standing and there was a burnt match on the ground where he had been standing, but he had disappeared entirely. Close behind where he had stood the woodland sloped steeply to a ravine filled with an almost impenetrable thicket of bushes and young trees, and even as I listened I seemed to hear the crackling of dry twigs below and to the right. But although I searched everywhere, I found no trace of the man with the gray suit, and I was forced to class him with the other unsolved mysteries of Laurelcrest.

That afternoon Mrs. St. John spent with her husband. Whether he believed her story of a headache sufficient to keep her away from his room for forty-eight hours, I do not know, but it is certain that through all the network of falsehood and equivocation that surrounded him, and of which he was partly aware, his faith in her never swerved. He watched her with the same loving, compassionate eyes, and welcomed her faintest smile as if he never suspected her of deceiving him. I came through my experiences at Laurelcrest with one strong desire— to be some day as good a man, as true and loyal a gentleman as Harry St. John. When my practice crowds me, as it sometimes does now, and I find myself irritable with anxiety and overwork, I pull myself together with a backward glance at the days when he faced death with composure and fought for his wife's well-being to what he knew was the verge of the grave.

Things seemed to have assumed a normal condition again. With the escape of the prisoner I imagined that the mystery would clear up, that there would be an end to the noise in the cellar and the tower lights; that Mrs. St. John would be her own smiling self, and that St. John could go to his operation with a mind free at least of other anxieties, which shows exactly how little we know of the future.

I was more complacent that afternoon than I had been since my arrival at Laurelcrest. For one thing I began to believe that Ellis was a less formidable rival than I had feared. Hotchkiss had been nearly right when he had declared that there was contempt in Georgia's eyes when she looked at her fiancé. I did not think that, but I was beginning to see that there was no love. I did not deceive myself, however; that she did not love Ellis did not imply that she cared at all for me. In fact, I could not remember the slightest encouragement to think she even liked me, but so inconsequential a thing is twenty-six that on no grounds at all I began to dream exceedingly silly but exceedingly enchanting dreams, in which the big mahogany breakfast table at Laurelcrest shrank to smaller dimensions, with places laid for two, and behind the coffee urn was a face with reddish brown hair and black, finely drawn brows over frank blue eyes.

In view of the approaching operation, I set down to work that afternoon to study my brain surgery text. But I read little. Instead, I watched Georgia and Ellis walking slowly back and forth along the drive, he in earnest conversation, while she said little, and walked with her eyes on the ground before her. After a bit I slammed the book into a corner and putting on a topcoat went out into the air. I met Georgia coming in and was horrified to see tears in her eyes. She spoke to me coolly and went into the house. Then I went out—to the greatest surprise of all.

Ellis was still pacing the drive, his hands in his pockets, his face scowling. At my approach he looked up with an attempt at civility, and I surmised that I had witnessed the termination of a lovers' quarrel. Perhaps I found some satisfaction in the thought; certainly Ellis was the picture of anything but a successful lover, and just as certainly he wished me anywhere but beside him. I had a definite purpose, however, in finding him out, and after a few desultory remarks about the weather, and a similar number of grudging monosyllables, I broached the subject.

"I'd like to have a little talk with you, Ellis," I said. "It's about Mr. St. John, and perhaps I would better say that I am consulting you at Mr. Wheatly's request."

"Fire away," he said brusquely, "though I don't think Harry St. John would approve of my being consulted about his affairs."

"Perhaps not," I assented. "I can't say that I am very anxious to do it either, but it comes by elimination. We cannot consult with his wife, for certain reasons, and you are her nearest relative. It is only a form, really, for I do not believe your disapproval would affect the case at all; just the same, I hope you will see the thing as we do."

"Well, what is it?" he cried impatiently. "What is this subject about which I am to be consulted, and about which my opinion will make no difference?"

I told him then. I told him of St. John's present hopeless condition, of his anxiety to keep it from his wife, and of the chance now offered for recovery, and the risk it involved. I was so interested in putting my case that I had not noticed its effect on Ellis. When I finally looked up I was struck with the expression on his face. He was white even around the lips, and he stopped walking to look at me with horror-filled eyes.

"And he may recover," he said with difficulty. "He may get around again, and learn—why, it's impossible; Dr. Jamieson told me so."

"Jamieson is an ass," I said irritably. "Anyhow, I should think common decency would make you at least express a hope for the success of the operation. He's your sister's husband, and you look as if the prospect of his recovery is the last thing on earth you desire."

"It is," he half-whispered. "It—it will be a calamity, nothing less." He looked furtively toward the house, then turned to me again, his black eyes no longer shifting, but blazing fiercely with some emotion I could not fathom. "It cannot be, doctor," he said, almost fiercely. "I tell you there are reasons why that operation must not occur."

"They would have to be very convincing reasons," I said, trying to keep my temper. "It will take more than generalities to stop things now."

He looked at me as if he could have struck me; then he thought better of it.

"I'll give you a reason," he said, "that will make you think twice before you bring Harry St. John back to life that would be worse than death. You know him pretty well; you know what he thinks of his wife. Would life be worth anything to him, do you think, if he learned that his wife is at intervals hopelessly insane?"

My first thought was intense disbelief followed by an uneasy consciousness that at least the thing was possible. What about the handkerchief at the foot of the dumbwaiter shaft? What of Mrs. St. John's many headaches, when she shut herself in her room and refused medicine? What of the injuries to her arm and the blood on Georgia Ellis's sleeve? What about the woman at the tower window? Was not even her sudden refusal to come to Laurelcrest a sign of some mental disorder? Hotchkiss himself had suggested the possibility of a woman in the tower room.

After all, it must be true. It would account for Georgia Ellis's connection with the case and—I stopped suddenly in my walk and looked toward the public road which wound past the foot of the lawn, two or three hundred yards away. A solitary horseman was passing slowly along, looking intently in our direction. Horsemen in the vicinity were not rare—the roads were too poor for vehicles—but they were ordinarily of the usual type of native. There was something different about this man. and I felt a conviction that this gray-suited rider was the man in similar clothes I had seen in the shadow of the woods. When I turned to speak to Ellis, however, he was gone, walking rapidly toward the house, and I was convinced that his hasty departure was due to the man on the road. Had I really learned the solution of the mystery after all, or was I as I had been before, involved in a tissue of falsehood and mystery which left me doubting everyone, even the girl I loved?

CHAPTER SIXTEEN

It was Tuesday afternoon when Ellis and I talked together in the garden. Until Friday things moved smoothly enough. Nothing transpired either to prove or disprove his assertion about his sister, and after careful debate Hotchkiss and I decided to allow the operation to proceed. It would have been difficult to do anything else, and after all, who were we, to juggle with a man's chance for life, on the bald and unauthenticated statement of another man? If Mrs. St. John was insane, as seemed probable, there was the more need of a protector for her. If Ellis lied, then there was needed someone with a strong hand and the authority to tear aside the false and reveal the truth.

Thursday afternoon I gave Ellis some morphia. He seemed excited and anxious, and while he did not say so, he intimated the approach of another outbreak of insanity in his sister. I had a small tube only partly filled with quarter-grain tablets, and I gave him about four, warning him to be careful. He reminded me, curtly, that he had put in a couple of years at a medical college and that he knew the danger. He turned and went out then. I was preparing to study, when he came back. "Look here, Pierce," he said, "is the operation going to take place?"

"It is."

"When?"

"When Dr. Carter and his assistant get here, at ten o'clock on Friday."

He seemed to ponder over the information for a few minutes. When he spoke it was with less of constraint than he had shown to me in recent days.

"I wish you would arrange to let me be there," he said. "I know—frankly—what you think of me. But now that you know why I am here, can't you stretch a point and let me in? I could help, you know—run for things, fix hypodermics, anything. Can you work it?"

"I don't know," I said slowly. "Carter's querulous about some things. But it wouldn't hurt to have some member of Mrs. St. John's family present. Suppose you get ready, and if I can arrange it with Carter, I will."

I felt a little uneasy about the arrangement, but it was up to Carter now, and after all, considering the nature of the operation, an extra assistant might be badly needed.

I was somewhat puzzled during those last days by Hotchkiss. He was rarely at home; took to missing meals unaccountably and to coming in late at night. What hurt me more than anything, however, was his reticence to me.

"You've got your work cut out for you," he said cheerfully. "This is something in my line. All I want you to do is to bring Harry through safely; if you do that, I'll clear up my end about the same time, and we'll be a kind of plural guardian angel to the St. Johns."

I had to be satisfied with that. In other ways, however, things went more smoothly. Georgia was no longer cold and constrained, and there were no more long walks and talks with Ellis. But while I gained in some ways I had lost in others. She seemed to avoid being alone with me, and when she was would sit for hours over a bit of embroidery, which she had confessed once that she loathed, while I talked or read to her. We read the romantic poets, I remember; and to this day there are certain lines that bring before me the picture of a girl in a soft blue gown, sewing in the shade of a big lamp while from somewhere in the background Ellis's black eyes scowl at us.

Mrs. St. John went about like a pale, white ghost. She spent much time with her husband, and the last day or two I thought she began to recognize the seriousness of his condition. Once she tried to speak to me about it, but her lips quivered when she tried to talk, and with her handkerchief to her eyes she went out. It was a gloomy household. I seem to remember nothing but tears and sobs during those last few days, and there were times when the atmosphere pressed on me so that I would put on my coat and take a brisk walk through the woods, listening to the crisp crackle of leaves under my feet, and wishing with all my heart that I could take the girl I loved away to some sunny, cheerful spot where people were actuated by natural motives, and where locked rooms and midnight shrieks were things read of in penny thrillers.

By Friday evening everything was ready. Miss Martin was hustling with suppressed excitement, anxious to get Mrs. St. John away, so she could prepare her patient, and afraid to arouse suspicion by driving her out. The packages of sterilized dressings and other necessaries had been smuggled from Carson by Hotchkiss and lay, ready for use, in Miss Martin's room. I had secured a powerful electric lamp with a reflector, which needed only to be slipped into place, and having robbed the linen-closet of dozens of towels, we were in some measure prepared, I as pretty nervous myself by ten o'clock. St. John was the calmest of the three; except that his good night to his wife was rather lingering, he might have been expecting to have been read quietly to sleep as on other nights. Mrs. St. John went away as she was told, almost childishly docile, and I walked down the corridor with her. Her evening gown had sleeves cut to the elbow, and I noticed what I had not seen before. The bandage was gone, and there was a long, red, irregular scar on the white flesh of her forearm. I was suddenly filled with pity for her; negative as she had seemed in character, it seemed to me the hopelessness of a spirited woman, whose spirit was broken, not the smoldering fire of a maniac, ready to burst out at any moment.

Hotchkiss met Carter and Charlie Atkinson and drove them to the house. There, as before, I met them, and we slipped softly to the entrance in the west wing and up the stairs.

St. John was calmness itself. He shook hands with the men, and I think his paramount sensation at that moment was that he was glad the long wait was over. Miss Martin hustled around, getting hot water, fixing trays, bringing towels, and fixing lights, her face pale with excitement. Even Atkinson, who generally anesthetizes for Carter, felt the infection of the unusual circumstances, and for my part I could hear my heart beating in my ear drums.

To my relief, Ellis had not appeared. He had gone for a walk that afternoon and I had not seen him since. Hotchkiss had taken the team around to the stables and the arrangement was that later he should mount guard in the hallway. By the time things were ready, however, he had not come, and Atkinson had arranged his chloroform and oxygen apparatus ready to begin, before I heard a step outside. It was Ellis, however, and even in the excitement of the moment I noticed his unusual appearance. He was muddy and disheveled, and his face was a sickly yellow-white. He shook hands with Carter, mumbling something about assisting and Carter looked at me.

My explanation seemed satisfactory, but Carter's brows were slightly raised, and he told him to hold himself in readiness to assist, but that he did not think he would need him.

There was nothing sensational about St. John. He took the chloroform quietly, raising the mask once as the fumes came a little strong, but breathing slowly and deeply until his relaxed hand dropped to his side and he slept.

For the next ten minutes the room was perfectly quiet. Carter worked busily, his eyes frowning intently, the black hair dropping over his forehead.

Atkinson, seated at the head of the bed, gave the chloroform, not taking his hand from his patient's pulse. I handed instruments which Miss Martin washed and sterilized in an improvised sterilizer, while in a corner Ellis, now duly aproned like the rest of us, watched and sulked.

Then something happened. There was a sudden rush, a shriek, a twisting of tangled bodies beside the bed, and a crash as the instrument stand went over. 1 caught a glimpse of a purplish, distorted face, which was Ellis, and of Carter fighting to retain the knife he held in his hand. As Carter went down with a crash, I was over the bed, clutching at the knife, which Ellis now flourished, missing, clutching again, my fingers cut to the bone, blood streaming over everything; while again and again Ellis lunged past me at the unconscious figure on the bed.

Atkinson had got to my aid then, but even with his help we could not hold the frenzied man with the knife. Once I felt a red-hot stab of pain in my shoulder, where the knife went home, and I was conscious of tramping, now and then, on Carter's unconscious form. Finally, I got my leg around one of Ellis's and succeeded in throwing him. He fell heavily, and as I went down with him I had a blurred vision of the door violently flung open and admitting two or three men. I knocked my head on something and lay half stunned for a minute. When I came around Carter had got to his feet, still white and with a jagged cut on his temple, while Hotchkiss and two strange men were carrying Ellis, securely handcuffed, from the room.

From the corridor Mrs. St. John and Georgia stood huddled together, Mrs. St. John was livid, and she watched the little procession with wide, horrified eyes. As it came near her she sank to her knees with a groan, and then Carter banged the door and I saw nothing more.

"Now that's settled," he said coolly, wiping the blood from his forehead. "We'll go on with this thing. Ready, Atkinson?"

I tied up my bleeding hands with Miss Martin's assistance and the operation proceeded as if nothing had occurred. At the end of twenty minutes Carter's face began to clear, and at the end of a half-hour he looked up with a smile.

"I always said Jamieson was an ass," he said triumphantly, as he reached for a bandage. "Now I know it."

When everything was over Carter gave me a little attention, putting in a stitch here and there with a grim smile when I flinched. Then while Miss Martin cleared the room we waited around St. John's bed, waiting for the first signs of returning consciousness. He was long in recovering, but at the last he moved his arms uneasily and muttered something inarticulate.

Carter leaned over and watched him carefully. But the real triumph was mine, for just as dawn was stealing through the windows I pointed to the bed. St. John was slowly, cautiously, moving his paralyzed leg.

CHAPTER SEVENTEEN

The operation being over, all need of secrecy was gone. We breakfasted together, Hotchkiss, Carter, Atkinson and I, and I learned the meaning of what had happened the night before.

Hotchkiss was beaming and was too exultant to care for food, but I noticed Saunders was pale and uneasy and I surmised that some of the night's events had made their way into the kitchen.

"It's rather a long story," Hotchkiss said. "I suppose, Dr. Carter, that Pierce has told you what he knows—of the locked tower room, of our adventures in the cellar and of Ellis's statement that his sister was insane was an argument against the operation?"

"Yes. I've told him all I know," I interposed.

"Well, a couple of days ago, driving home from Carson, I came unexpectedly across a man on horseback, who had stopped his horse down the road a bit, and was watching the house sharply."

"Did he wear a gray suit?" I asked.

"Yes. I came on him unexpectedly and he looked uncomfortable. But he made the best of it. 'Pretty place, isn't it?' he said and tried to get past me. 'I don't know much about beauty,' I said, but I've seen you admiring that place for over two or three days at a distance, and if I were you and wanted information, I'd ask for it. There may be people there who could tell you things.' Well, it ended with my making an appointment to meet him that night, when we would be less conspicuous, and have a talk. I didn't even tell you, Pierce, for you were worried enough about Harry. But I learned that Ellis, who has been subject for several years to attacks of violent murderous frenzy, had quite recently during one of these killed a man in his home city, a livery stable keeper, braining him with a chair and escaping to his sister afterward. The detective, whose name is Adams, said that he lost trace of him entirely until a day or so ago, and when he did find him he waited to send to the city for help; it promised to be a two-men job to get him. When I drove around to the stables last night I found Adams and the new man, and it was lucky that I did."

Carter and I were looking rather used up. Carter had a blue spot on the tip of his chin and a cut on the temple, while I had my wrists and hands done up in bandages, with a shoulder so stiff that I could not lift my arm. But we were rather a gay crowd than otherwise. With Carter there was the consciousness of work well done, while Hotchkiss had been in the most exciting capture of his career, and I—I tried to eat, tried to be sorry for this, tried for the sake of composure to forget that Georgia was free again, but uselessly. I tried to escape from the interminable meal, only to be called back.

"You can go in a minute," Hotchkiss said dryly. "This story of mine is newer than the story you want to tell." So I subsided sulkily into a chair and listened.

"It has been a fortunate thing for Harry's wife that these two things happened together. She is so anxious about her husband now that her brother's capture is of secondary importance. The whole thing has been a case of mistaken kindness. She has always shielded him during his attacks of insanity, and so far she has kept him out of an asylum. But when he came to her a month ago, with the story of accidentally killing a man, she was at her wits' end. She sent him here, Georgia tells me, with a male nurse, who posed as a valet, and who had the tower room fixed as we found it. But Ellis nearly killed this fellow and he left, taking the other servants with him.

"When St. John persisted in coming here his wife was almost frantic. She sent up new servants, and because she and Georgia were afraid of another attack on a nurse, they essayed to look after him themselves. It was more than they had counted on. Ellis, during his two years at medical college, began to use morphia, and it was to get morphia that he visited the car on the side track, Pierce. It was morphia that Georgia took from Miss Martin's tray that night, and it was morphia again in the pink box which Georgia accidentally gave you instead of the yellow. She and Harry's wife had a terrible fright that night, I can tell you."

"And the shriek in the tower?" I asked.

"Was Mrs. St. John. Ellis attacked both women and they barely escaped. He cut Mrs. St. John on her arm with a knife from his supper-tray, much as we surmised, and without noticing the blood on her sleeve, Georgia came down to allay your suspicions. Then, the night we were in the cellar, Ellis slid down the rope and escaped. When I saw him running across the lawn he was pursued, not the pursuer."

"Now I understand the way the dumbwaiter was nailed down," I said suddenly; "I might have known a woman had driven those nails. And St. John, knowing of these attacks of insanity, would never have permitted him here, and for that reason was kept in ignorance?"

"Exactly."

"Well, it's a strange case," said Carter, preparing to rise. "You talk all you like about the excitement of city life, but for pure, unadulterated hair-raising business, give me the heart of the mountains, a night's journey from town and an hour from a newspaper. Here we find under our roof insanity, attempted murder, assault and battery and a modern surgical operation, all mixed with a cement of fear and mystery."

"There is love, too," said Hotchkiss, slyly looking at me.

"I believe you know, Mr. Hotchkiss," I said. And he had the grace to blush.

They took Ellis away that morning, still raving mildly. And Georgia and I together watched the carriage go down the drive. As it disappeared, she drew a long breath of relief.

"It has been terrible for you," I said, with a sudden realization that she was very white and tired. "Harder for you than for anyone, since you expected to marry him."

"I broke the engagement two years ago," she said, "but he wouldn't release me and I—I was afraid."

"But you cared for him," I said, with the old jealousy flaming again. "You were only afraid to marry him."

She smiled tolerantly. "One does not love a maniac," she said.

Far away under the trees were two figures, well wrapped from the wind. They were walking rapidly, Hotchkiss a little ahead, Miss Martin trying heroically to keep up. Even as we looked the elderly lovers stopped and, after furtively looking around, Hotchkiss stooped gallantly and kissed the lady's hand.

I looked at Georgia. She was smiling, and with a sudden impulse I took the small hand that hung listless at her side and kissed it twice.

"I'm afraid I'm bungling, as usual," I said, as I still held it, "but somehow this thing won't keep. I'm not worthy of you, Georgia, but I love you with all my heart, and some day when I have won my spurs, I'm coming back to ask you to marry me. Shall I come?"

"Yes, come," she whispered, and I kissed her.

ABOUT THE AUTHOR

Mary Roberts Rinehart (1876–1958) was one of the United States's most popular early mystery authors. Born in Pittsburgh to a clerk at a sewing machine agency, Rinehart trained as a nurse and married a doctor after her graduation from nursing school. She wrote fiction in her spare time until a stock market crash sent her and her young husband into debt, forcing her to lean on her writing to pay the bills. Her first two novels, *The Circular Staircase* (1908) and *The Man in Lower Ten* (1909), established her as a bright young talent, and it wasn't long before she was one of the nation's most popular mystery novelists.

Among her dozens of novels are *The Amazing Adventures of Letitia Carberry* (1911), which began a six-book series, and *The Bat* (originally published in 1920 as a play), which was among the inspirations for Bob Kane's Batman. Credited with inventing the phrase "The butler did it," Rinehart is often called an American Agatha Christie, even though she began writing much earlier than Christie, and was much more popular during her heyday.

MARY ROBERTS RINEHART

FROM MYSTERIOUSPRESS.COM
AND OPEN ROAD MEDIA

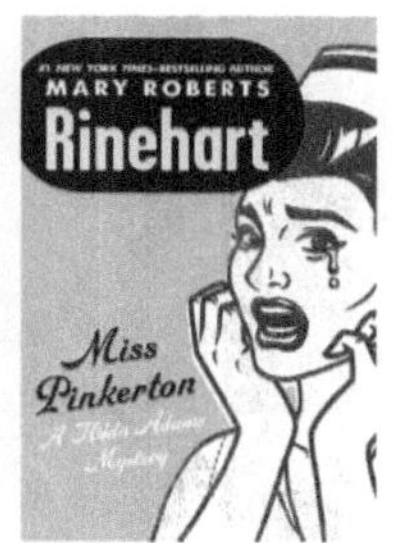
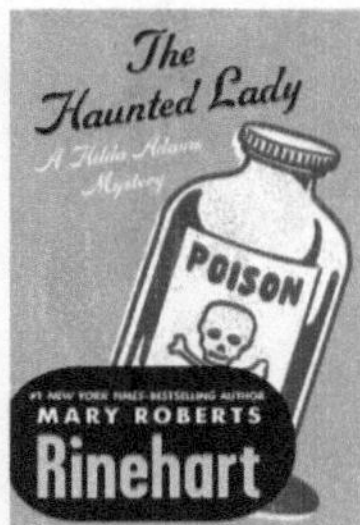

MYSTERIOUSPRESS.COM

THE MYSTERIOUS BOOKSHOP, founded in 1979, is located in Manhattan's Tribeca neighborhood. It is the oldest and largest mystery-specialty bookstore in America.

The shop stocks the finest selection of new mystery hardcovers, paperbacks, and periodicals. It also features a superb collection of signed modern first editions, rare and collectable works, and Sherlock Holmes titles. The bookshop issues a free monthly newsletter highlighting its book clubs, new releases, events, and recently acquired books.

58 Warren Street
info@mysteriousbookshop.com
(212) 587-1011
Monday through Saturday
11:00 a.m. to 7:00 p.m.

FIND OUT MORE AT:

www.mysteriousbookshop.com

FOLLOW US:

@TheMysterious and Facebook.com/MysteriousBookshop